THE ILLINOIS CAPER

THE ILLINOIS CAPER

Published by Rainy Valley Press, Salem, Oregon.

Library of Congress Control Number: 2023907130

ISBN trade paperback: 978-1-955720-00-7

ISBN e-book: 978-1-955720-01-4

Cover design by Kim Killion of Killion Publishing. https://thekilliongroupinc.com/

THE ILLINOIS CAPER

THE ROUTE 66 STEAL
BOOK ONE

LIZ HARTLEY

RAINY VALLEY PRESS

"…there is hope on the road…A sense of opportunity as wide as the country itself. A bone-deep conviction that something better will come. It's just ahead, in the next town, the next gig, the next chance encounter with a stranger."

Nomadland
Jessica Bruder

CONTENTS

CHAPTER 1
THE DECISIONS

The door hit the frame so hard it bounced back, slamming into the wall. The glass in their wedding photo shattered as it crashed to the floor.

Tish O'Donnell grabbed the rebounding door, slammed it again, and threw the deadbolt.

"Don't come sniveling back, either!" she shouted at the still-shuddering wood.

He would of course. His name was on the mortgage.

And he'd bring *her*.

She spun around and caught a glimpse of herself in the hall mirror: pale skin blotched with anger, dark brown eyes blazing in a soft, round face. Her gray-shot red hair, piled high, was askew.

Like Rochester's mad wife in Jane Eyre, she thought. She'd loved that book as a girl, but she'd always seen herself as strong, competent Jane, not this...this wild-eyed creature that stared at her from the mirror's depths.

"Urrrgh!" she growled in rage. Her fists clenched with the urge to hit something.

Heedless of the crunching glass underfoot, Tish stormed back through the foyer toward the kitchen, kicking an enameled, cast-iron saucepan out of the way.

"Shit! Shoot!" she shouted, correcting quickly and hopping as pain shot up her foot. "I'll kill you, you ba…"

She hesitated fractionally, but no word that would not result in penance suggested itself.

"You…schmuck!" she yelled at the walls. As if God didn't understand Yiddish. She limped into the kitchen, turned a chair upright and sat down, and pulled off her shoe to massage her insulted toes.

Yiddish or not, it still meant more Hail Marys. Father Andrew didn't allow cursing, even in a situation like this. He didn't overlook it if it was in Yiddish, either. She'd tried that argument before.

The image of a divine frown couldn't stop the stream of profanities going through her mind, though. God would just have to understand.

Fear of celestial disapproval wasn't slowing Fitz down, she thought bitterly. Oh, no. It didn't stop him from saying the "d" word.

Not after thirty-five years, she fumed, rubbing her stockinged foot. *Not after thirty-five long, hard years, three kids, and constant humiliation. You're not leaving me with nothing. Not now. Just because you think you're "in love" with your current piece of…flesh.*

"Not for that scheming…" The "b" word hovered on her lips, but the last hour had already given her too much to confess.

"…trollop," was what she settled for.

Kat Merevec. With her tight ass and her big, pointy tits and her purple hair. It had to be her, though she'd always thought Kat was smarter than that. Though why Kat should be any different, Tish didn't know. Fitz had screwed every store manager they'd had for the last thirty-five years.

Almost all. Ted had been the exception.

He'd slept with them all—and others besides.

But he'd never left her to marry any of them.

"You wait until her boobs head south, you miserable... loser!" she shouted at the door down the hall. "See how much you 'love' her then. See how much she 'loves' *you* when you're broke and selling bead bracelets from a ratty blanket in Fountain Square. Because believe me, you two-timing mongrel, when I'm done with you, you'll have to start over again. Fancy doing *that* at your age?"

It should have been my business, not his, she thought bitterly. But her father had given it to Fitz on their wedding day. Because Fitz was the *man. Men* had heads for business, he'd said, not girls.

Girls.

She'd been hurt. Outraged. Furious. Her father, chuckling, had just patted her on the cheek and left it to Fitz to sooth and assure her.

"It's *ours*, sweetie. Together. It's *our* business." Or home. Or retirement. It was always "ours."

Except, of course, that everything was in *his* name.

Even *their* cars were in *his* name.

Except, of course, for that gas hog, the only thing her father had given her. Fitz had started saying it reminded him of her. "It's got a front end and back end as big as yours," he'd laugh. When she'd glower, he'd just pat her bottom and say, "Honey, I'm teasing. You know I love all of you."

Har. Har.

Yet despite it all, despite the loss of the business, despite the cheating Fitz had done over the years, she'd stuck it out.

She'd believed him when he said it was all theirs. She'd *needed* to believe him, because without belief, she had nothing.

But Tish didn't believe any more.

Her mind began ticking over as her white-hot anger cooled to cherry red.

When I'm done with you, she thought.

Who was she kidding? How could she hurt *him*?

She'd get screwed in a divorce. She knew it. All her friends had gotten screwed. Why should she be any different?

The first time Tish had discovered Fitz's infidelity, they'd only been married a few months. Tish hadn't even turned twenty. Her mother had shrugged it off. All men ran around, she said. Tish was married. Make the best of it.

The priest said divorce wasn't possible. Marriage was forever. He'd speak to Fitz. Think of the children to come.

So, Tish thought of the children, and she made the best of it. She worked in the store that should have been hers. Closed her eyes when Fitz cheated.

Eventually she convinced herself that other women were nuts for leaving when their husbands had affairs. Everyone knew that women lived longer than men. It would all be yours if you just waited them out.

That thought, and making herself a very expensive piece of jewelry every time Fitz found a 'new love,' had helped ease the pain.

But now...this.

Not on your pitiful, useless life, Fitzpatrick O'Donnell. You are not divorcing Mary Patrice Geraghty Ryan.

Not without a fight.

When I'm done with you, she thought again.

And paused...as a terrible idea crossed her mind.

A terrible, beautiful, brilliant idea.

Tish's lips curled in a smile that would have scared Fitz's socks off if he'd been there to see it.

She stood up, shoved her throbbing foot back into her shoe, grabbed her keys and purse, and headed for the garage.

When I'm done with you, she thought with relish, *you can have the* damned *house and the* damned *store.*

And I'll make Father Andrew's hair stand on end.

Across town, Kat Merevec stood motionless, arms crossed, staring out the bedroom window of her leased condo in a relatively new complex on the edge of Evanston, Illinois. She didn't know how long she'd been staring into the night, watching the darkness thicken. She didn't remember coming to stand there.

She only remembered the humiliation. The fury.

They burned in her throat.

Occasionally her deep blue eyes flickcd—left, then right —tracking the lights in the complex as they blinked off, one by one. Now only the porch lights remained lit.

Porch lights, she thought, her first conscious thought in what? Hours? *A gated, guarded community. Every house with alarms and cameras. Hourly patrols. And they leave porch lights on like frightened children.*

What on earth was she doing here?

How had she ended up like this? With a management job, a bland, beige condo in a bland, beige neighborhood, and some kind of generic vehicle. She, Kat Merevec, who could practically tell the difference between two cars that rolled off the assembly line moments apart, could never remember what make it was. Something gray. Impossible to find in parking lots.

She hadn't loved a car since the 1968 VW Bug she and her father had rebuilt and rebuilt until they couldn't rebuild it anymore.

How had that girl ended up trapped here?

Disgusted with herself.

Alone.

Scared.

The late May air coming in the open window was balmy, but Kat, her arms wrapped around herself, was cold. She dragged a brightly embroidered red wool shawl—the only color in the room—from the chair next to her and pulled it around her shoulders for comfort as well as warmth. She automatically pushed the large-framed, black glasses up her nose, then went back to watching the night.

As the stars moved across the sky, she unconsciously began to tap her right middle finger against her arm.

The bastard, she thought. *All I asked for was a little help. A little support. A little goddamned show of concern!*

She'd never loved him, for pity's sake. She knew he certainly had never loved her. But she'd managed Superior Jewelers for him for six years, and they'd slept together for almost six weeks. He could have at least *pretended* something this important mattered to him.

Instead, when she'd stood in his office that afternoon, and asked for his help, he'd barely acknowledged her words, before he'd told her that it was all for the best anyway. That he'd found the love of his life, and he was starting over fresh.

In view of the circumstances, he'd told her, it was best if she just left at the end of the day and didn't come back to the store.

Just like that she'd lost her job.

Her income.

Her health insurance.

Just like that, his promises vanished...like steam off a fresh pile of cow shit.

He'd put her final check in the mail to her on Tuesday, he said, after the Memorial Day weekend. "Don't worry," he'd added, patting her cheek and tempting her to bite his finger off, "I'll add a nice little bonus to it. After all. It's the least I can do."

In view of the circumstances...

And the son of a bitch had winked. Winked!

The least he could do.

Damn straight it was the *least* he could do.

Then his phone had rung, and he'd gotten a smarmy look on his face. "We'll finish this later," he'd said, turned away, and murmured, "Yes, my sweetness?" into the phone as he went to sit behind his desk.

Kat had wanted to throw up on one of his leather chairs.

Instead, she'd held it together, walked out of his office, and out of the store, with the keys still in her purse. Because if there was one thing she knew about Fitz O'Donnell, it was that—besides being a cheat—he was a liar.

He'd already taken her future away from her. There was no way this side of hell she'd turn over her store keys to him, not until she had her check—and a considerable bonus—in hand. She'd seen what his "promises" meant. Those keys were the only leverage she had to make sure she got this, at least.

Fitz wouldn't want to spend money changing the locks. He was nothing if not a cheapskate. She'd expected him to call to demand them back, but he hadn't. Obviously caught up in his new "love," he'd forgotten she had them.

Tish wouldn't have forgotten, if she'd been working. But then, Tish had her own problems now.

Six years. Countless promises. Now, nothing.

How could she have been so stupid?

Too easily.

She was forty-five years old and had a great body that she worked hard to keep, much good that would do her now. She had nothing else. No real home. No family. She wanted roots. She wanted something that was *hers*. She wanted a *place*.

Now she didn't even have her job.

Dark visions of her future flicked through her imagination, edged with the red of her blazing anger. Still, Kat remained motionless, the volcanic churning of her mind visible only in the constant tapping of her middle finger.

One flame-threaded thought kept pushing itself forward. She consciously considered it, expecting to find it ludicrous. And it was.

She pushed it aside.

It came back.

She examined it again.

The more she thought about it, the less ludicrous it became.

Until she smiled.

"*A little bonus,*" he'd said. A little something extra to ease her and her problem out the door.

A little bonus.

Kat thought for a while longer. Then she shoved her glasses back to the bridge of her nose, turned from the window and began to prepare.

CHAPTER 2

THE HEIST, PART ONE

Tish's hand shook as she unlocked the back door to the jewelry store. She'd opened this door thousands of times, but tonight it was different. She wasn't having second thoughts. Not exactly. Still... It was after midnight, and downtown Evanston, Illinois, was quiet. If she was caught, this would be hard to explain. Even if it was *their* store.

She thought of Fitz having all this. Of *her* having all this.

She yanked the door open.

Inside, she quickly moved to the opposite wall of the darkened workshop where the alarm was shrieking a warning. She punched in the code, and the red flashing light went to green.

Silence.

It was strange for the shop to be quiet. Normally it was filled with the cacophony of air compressors, the grating of saw blades on gold, the whirring electric motors, the tapping of hammers on silver, the hum of fans sucking out the fumes of overheated metal, burning wax, and baking rubber.

She picked up a brooch sketch on a nearby work bench. Tish's design. The one she knew the client would gush over. The one Fitz would claim credit for.

For a moment, grief overwhelmed her. This was where she belonged. *She* was the one who kept the books. *She* designed the jewelry and worked with the setters and goldsmiths. *She* ordered product.

Okay, sure. Fitz was a champion schmoozer, holding the wealthy women's hands in his soft fingers with their polished nails, understanding them when their husbands didn't (what a joke!), and designing jewelry—just for them. Of course, it always came down to Tish, working with their leading goldsmith, Baruch, to save the design. Like the one in her hand. But would Fitz ever give her credit?

Gently she laid the drawing back down.

After her father had died, she'd tried to get Fitz to put her name on the business, make her a partner. She'd even tried to be diplomatic. All she'd gotten in response was, "But sweetie. It's already *ours*."

Her resolve turned to iron.

Tish moved to the front of the silent store and looked out the curved glass double front doors and two walls of display windows (all shatterproof glass) to downtown Evanston where only a few cars rolled by. Over the years, her father had bought up the leases of the stores along the streets adjacent to their corner location. Finally, he'd bought the building. It was the biggest independent jewelry store in the greater Chicago area.

Though they still carried a few lines of porcelain and glass statuary and gift items, most of the showroom was filled with jewelry cases, now empty. It took more than an hour for staff to set them up every morning, taking all the jewelry from the vault, polishing away the fingerprints, brushing the velveteen displays and pads so they looked pristine, putting all the gold back on display. Tish hated the task. She'd always hated it.

Well, she'd cleaned her last case.

She crossed the showroom to Fitz's office. The throne room, Tish always called it, even when it had been her father's. It had annoyed both him and Fitz. They didn't need the huge space, the enormous desk, the recessed lighting, and the (reproduction) antiques in the alcoves around the walls, but it made them feel successful. Powerful.

Narcissistic idiots, both of them.

The wall of sliding closet doors opposite Fitz's desk were mirrored, making the room look even bigger. Fitz would preen in front of them whenever he was on the phone, fondling his moustache, touching his carefully colored hair (he thought she didn't know), tapping the gold-plated letter opener on the desk blotter. The big man. The important player.

She snorted.

She slid one of the doors open. Behind it squatted a large, black safe—the kind that had given rise to the term "safe cracker" because it could be opened by hitting it with a sledgehammer.

The finished jewelry and the everyday gemstones—the commercial grade stones, the ones they most often sold—were all kept in the vault, the large, state-of-the-art vault with the time lock on it, that sat in a special alcove off the showroom floor. In the office safe, Fitz kept the daily receipts, before the bank deposit was made, and in a zippered bag, he kept an additional $10,000 to $20,000 in cash to buy gold and platinum jewelry off the street.

Dumb enough.

But irrationally, the big black safe was also where Fitz kept the large, fine gemstones—those that only their top customers could afford—under his close personal supervision. He wanted to know when one of the staff took out a large diamond or a suite of fine sapphires to show a customer. He liked knowing how much money he might be making. He liked moving in on the salesperson at the end and claiming credit for the sale.

Tish suspected Fitz's ego also needed the reassurance of being able to pull the gemstones out any time he wanted. Many times, she'd caught him simply going through the stone boxes, unfolding the individual papers and looking at the stones in their soft batting nests. It wasn't because he loved their beauty. It was because he loved their value.

For years, Tish had talked herself dry, telling him to keep the stones in the vault where they would be safer. Fitz had refused. He insisted on having the stones where he could watch them.

Well, he wasn't watching now.

Tish smiled. This was going to be fun.

She played the flashlight over the front of the safe. She reached for the dial.

"I guess I know what you're doing," said a voice behind her.

CHAPTER 3

THE HEIST, PART TWO

Tish leaped and spun. The light from the flashlight flailed around the room and came to a jittery halt on Kat's face, reflecting from her large-lensed, black-framed glasses. She was standing in the doorway dressed in black, her purple hair covered with a black knit cap.

"I can't say I'm surprised," said Kat. She *was* surprised, however, by how calm her own voice was, considering she felt like she was in free fall, finding Tish here.

Sometimes her whole life felt like she was in free fall.

Tish's mouth moved, but it was a moment before words came out. "What the *hell* are you doing here?" she finally managed to ask.

Kat hesitated slightly. "I was jogging past. I saw the light. Thought I'd better see that all was secure."

A look of panic crossed Tish's face. Then her eyes narrowed.

"No, you didn't," she said. "This is a penlight. And the office door doesn't face the street."

Kat shrugged. It had been worth a try.

"So, what are you really doing here? In the middle of the night?" asked Tish.

"Why are *you* here?" countered Kat.

"It's my store."

"Oh? Is that why it says 'Fitzpatrick J. O'Donnell, prop.' under 'Superior Jewelers' on the window?" said Kat, taking a risk and prodding a sensitive spot. She'd heard Tish arguing to have Fitz make her a partner. She waved a black-gloved hand. "Get that thing out of my face. We're on the same side after all."

Tish lowered the light.

"Same side?" said Tish, her voice rising in anger. "*Same side*? You're taking my husband and you say we're on the same *side*?"

"Me? I'm not taking him," said Kat, making a sour face. Well, it wasn't *not* the truth.

"Bull...loney.

"Nope." Kat pulled off the knit cap and rubbed a hand through her spiky hair. "Nope, not me. He's marrying 'his one true love' and making a clean start."

"He dumped you?"

"He fired me." The bitterness in Kat's voice could have burned a hole in the carpet. "He said he was leaving you and making 'his true love' the new store manager."

Kat walked closer, catching the scent of Shalimar, the perfume Tish always wore.

Tish squinted at her, as if trying to decide whether to believe her or not. "So... If you're not the 'love he's been waiting for,' who is?"

"He didn't tell you?" Kat was surprised.

Tish shook her head. "I didn't give him much chance, between him saying 'divorce' and the first dish I threw at him."

"First?"

"So, who's he marrying?" Tish asked.

"Hilary."

"Hilary?"

"Yes. Hilary Shoenm…"

"Hilary the-goddamned-barista Shoenmeyer?"

Kat nodded.

"Hilary I'm-an-airhead-who-can't-spell-my-own-name Shoenmeyer? She can't be thirty!"

"She's twenty-five," said Kat.

"He's giving my store to that bi…that bimbo?" Tish's eyes almost stood out of her head. "Urrrgh!" She hit the safe with the side of her fist. "Ow!" She shook her hand out and looked back at Kat. "She can't even make a decent cup of coffee. At least you know how to run a store."

"Knew," said Kat.

"I wish I'd hit the son-of-a-…hound dog…with the Le Creuset," said Tish regretfully. "It might have killed him."

"You could have called me. I would have helped get rid of the body," said Kat.

"It's still an option," said Tish.

The two women looked at each other appraisingly for a few minutes.

"You still haven't said why you're here," said Tish, a bit more calmly.

"Same as you," said Kat. "Getting what I was promised."

"What you were promised?"

"My pay. My bonus. Fitz said he'd send them on Tuesday, but we both know Fitz isn't picky about the truth. I thought I'd pick up both now."

"Before he thought to change the locks and the combinations."

The hint of a smile curved Kat's mouth. "Same as you,"

she said again. "Aren't you here to get an advance on the divorce settlement you'll never see?"

Kat smiled broadly when Tish didn't deny it.

"Fitz always does underestimate the competition," she said.

"So, you expect me to pay you a bonus? Now? After you've broken into the store?" Tish asked. "In the middle of the night?"

Kat held up the keys. "I didn't break in. I'm store manager. I saw the light."

"No, you didn't."

Kat lifted her hands, palms up, and shrugged. "Maybe I didn't. So, call Fitz. Tell him I caught you in the office about to open the safe. You think he'll be so grateful you 'fessed up that he'll give up Hillary?"

Tish scowled at her, but Kat knew Tish was trapped.

They both were.

"So, what are you saying?" asked Tish.

"I suggest a deal."

"What kind of deal?" Tish asked warily.

Kat gestured to the safe. "We split what's in there, go our separate ways, and forget we ever saw each other."

"I don't think so," said Tish. "I have a right to be here. You've been fired."

"Not until Tuesday. And I really don't think Fitz would say you have a right to be here at..." Kat looked at her watch, "...one o'clock on a Sunday morning after he's told you that he's divorcing you."

"You're just an employee."

"Store manager. Who was passing and saw the light and thought I'd better check it out."

"You didn't."

Kat just smiled.

"As owner—co-owner—of the store, the courts will believe me."

Kat stepped to Fitz's desk and put her hand near the kneehole.

Panic danced across Tish's face.

"Let's call the police and see who they believe, shall we?" asked Kat, her hand hovering near the silent alarm button. "The wife who's been thrown over after more than thirty years, or the manager who is trying to stop a robbery from happening."

"A jilted lover, rather."

"So you say. I expect they'd call Fitz to sort it out, don't you?"

"Screw it," said Tish under her breath. "Yes, I expect they would. And the son-of-a...gopher would leave us both in jail to rot."

"And neither of us would get anything."

Tish glared.

"It's still my store."

"Fitz's name's on the door. You'll need to fight him in court for your share. Isn't it better to take it now? Leave the legal fees out of it?"

Kat watched as calculation washed the anger out of Tish's face. She saw the moment Tish changed her mind.

"So, what's to stop you from changing your mind later? Telling Fitz? Blackmailing me?" Tish asked.

"That would be an incredibly stupid move on my part," said Kat. "As it would be for you to say anything about me."

"Honor among thieves."

"Pretty much."

Tish thought a moment more. She was pretty sure there were more holes in this argument than a moth-eaten sweater, but she wanted the diamonds and other gemstones in the safe. Fitz could have everything else. The stones would give her a new start. A gem-encrusted bird in the hand...

If that meant trusting that Kat wouldn't turn on her later, well, she'd just have to chance it.

"I'll give you twenty-five percent," said Tish.

"Forty."

"Thirty-five."

"And the six-carat Kashmir," said Kat on impulse.

"You're out of your mind," said Tish. "That stone alone is worth..."

Kat's heart rate revved up. It had been a stab in the dark. But now Kat knew. Tish was after more than the cash.

The game had just changed.

"It's not to resell," said Kat, her voice calm. "It's for me. Like that Burmese ruby is for you."

Tish stopped.

"How did you kn...?"

"I've seen you look at it. I heard you argue with Fitz about giving it to you for your thirtieth anniversary."

"You don't even wear jewelry," said Tish.

"Sapphires are my birthstone."

Tish frowned.

"You've never mentioned that."

"No reason I would."

Kat didn't say that, from the moment she'd first seen it, the sapphire had called to her, its blue depths giving her peace.

Something she rarely felt any more.

She watched as Tish did the math in her head. Kat figured the other woman knew, to the penny, how much was in the safe.

Fitz is a fool to trade Tish for Hilary, she thought.

Slowly Tish nodded. But Kat was wary of the calculation still in Tish's eyes.

"Done. Come hold this." Tish held out the tiny flashlight.

Kat reached over and flipped on Fitz's desktop computer before she came around the desk to take the light. The blue screen lit up the room.

"Talk about seeing a light."

"I closed the office door," said Kat. She saw Tish's eyes flick across the room to be sure.

"Shine it on the dial," said Tish.

Kat did as she was asked.

Tish spun the dial to clear it, took a half a step back, and squinted,

"Are you serious?" asked Kat. "You came to open the safe and didn't bring your glasses?"

"I forgot, all right?" snapped Tish.

Kat held up a hand placatingly.

"Just asking," she said.

Tish glared at her and turned back to the dial. She squinted again.

Kat smothered her grin.

Tish rotated the dial swiftly right, then left, then right again and back to click. Shoved the handle down and pulled it toward her.

The massive door opened slowly.

Kat shone the light inside.

"Well, well. What's *that*?" she breathed.

CHAPTER 4
THE DISCOVERY

Kat eyed the large, worn, canvas duffel wedged into the bottom shelf of the safe in place of the trays of gold and platinum jewelry bought from the desperate people who would die of mortification before they went to a pawn shop. The bag was stuffed with something.

"You don't suppose it's...body parts...do you?" said Kat, only half facetiously.

Tish looked at her disdainfully. "You obviously don't know Fitz. It's probably dirty clothes. He may look like the cover of GQ, but at home the man is a slob. He'll go to any lengths to avoid putting clothes in the hamper."

"It wasn't in here yesterday," said Kat.

"You were in the safe yesterday?"

Kat shrugged. "I showed those one-carat diamonds to Mrs. Polanski. Again."

"She still didn't buy?"

Kat shook her head.

"That's like the fifth or sixth time, isn't it?" asked Tish.

"I've lost count. We should have been charging her a cover to come in the door and look."

Tish rolled her eyes. "Point the light over here."

Kat turned the flashlight on the small inner safe tucked into the upper third of the safe, like the freezer compartment in an old-fashioned refrigerator. It was where the larger, more valuable gemstones were kept.

Tish spun the dial to clear it.

"You know the combination?" Kat asked, casually, her heart hammering. *Decide. Decide!* she thought frantically. This was more than she'd planned on. "Fitz said no one knew it but him."

"I'm his wife," said Tish. "There's nothing I don't know. Fitz just thinks I don't know." She shot Kat a look. "How do you think I knew about you? And all the others."

Kat kept her face neutral. "You didn't know about Hilary, did you?"

"Just give me some light," snapped Tish, as she squinted, and turned the dial to the first number.

"I'm surprised it's not his birthday, like everything else," said Kat.

Tish stopped. Looked at Kat with speculation.

"You've tried to open this before?"

Kat looked back innocently. "It's not a big deal. I had a customer one day when you were both out of town at some show. She wanted to see some larger rubies." She gestured to the small inner compartment guarded by a dial. "I thought I could make the sale, so it was worth trying Fitz's birthday for the combination. After all, everything else is keyed to it."

Tish continued to stare at her.

"I lost the sale," said Kat, "because I couldn't open it. I couldn't believe there was another number he could remember." She didn't add that she'd also tried Tish's birthday, and each of the children's birthdays. "So, what makes this one special?"

Tish turned to manipulate the dial. "It's his mother's birthday," she said. "It's the only other date he can remember," she added under her breath as she dialed.

With the click of the final number, Tish pulled the small safe door open and froze.

Kat didn't notice. She was interested in the other items in the safe. She pushed Tish aside slightly and wrestled the duffel out of the small space where it was jammed. As she unzipped it, the dim light glinted from something behind the duffel.

"My, my, Fitz," she muttered.

She elbowed Tish.

"What?" said Tish, irritated, tearing her gaze from the inner safe.

Kat tipped her head toward the lower shelf. Tish looked down.

At the stack of gold ingots.

"What the hell?" said Tish. "Heck," she corrected automatically. "Where did those come from?"

"The old, dead inventory we pulled in March?" said Kat.

Every spring, Tish and Kat went through their inventory, took old or slow-moving stock out of inventory, and recycled it.

Tish shook her head. "That went to the refiners as scrap. I got their check the other day."

"Then what is this?" asked Kat. She frowned. "Could Baruch have made them?"

Tish pulled an ingot out. About the size of a military dog tag, only thicker, and stamped with "999.99 Fine Gold" and the store's hallmark, it lay on her palm and glowed, as only pure gold can.

The ultimate gold card.

"Why would Fitz have Baruch make ingots?" Tish wondered aloud. "We always buy our gold milled into sheet and wire, ready for use in the shop. We don't have any use for ingots."

"Something else you knew all about?"

"Shut up," said Tish testily.

She looked at Kat, who was stuffing the ingots into the duffel. "What are you doing? We can't take these. We can't get rid of them, not with our hallmark on them."

"We have to take them," said Kat. "What kind of burglars take diamonds and a bag of cash but not gold?"

"Cash?"

Kat held the duffel open to show Tish the stacks of hundred-dollar bills rubber-banded together.

"Jesus, Mary, and Joseph," breathed Tish. "What the hell is going on?" She didn't bother to correct herself.

Kat looked up sharply at the edge of panic in Tish's voice. "Why? What else is wrong?"

Tish pulled two stone boxes out of the inner safe. The long, narrow leatherette boxes that held the store's diamonds and fine gemstones were embossed with the store's logo. These boxes were worn and unmarked.

They didn't belong to Superior Jewelers.

Kat stared. "Those weren't there yesterday, either, when I got those diamonds to show Mrs. Polanski. The only stone boxes in there were ours."

She lifted one of the boxes from Tish's fingers, snapped the lid open, and pulled out a white stone paper. It was a bit grubby around the edges, and the handwriting on it was unfamiliar. Kat deftly unfolded the small envelope and the thin sheet of batting inside. Two diamonds, about three-quarters of a carat each, winked at her. In the poor light, Kat couldn't judge the quality.

The box was packed tightly with at least fifty or sixty stones. If they were all diamonds, and even if they were not the same quality as the stones in Superior's boxes...

The same thought was mirrored on Tish's face.

"I didn't count on this," said Tish, her voice quivering. "All I wanted were the stone boxes. And a fresh start."

"Now you have cash and gold, too, and we both have a fresh start," said Kat recovering quickly. She realized she'd made up her mind, and there was no going back.

Kat folded the paper in her hands, tucked it back into the box, and shut it. She took the other box out of Tish's unresisting hand and stuck them both in the duffel. "Get the others," she said, and finished filling the duffel.

Tish pulled Superior's three stone boxes—two filled with diamonds, one filled with colored stones—from the interior safe, and handed them to Kat, who zipped them into the duffel.

"Leave the safe the way it is. Let's go," said Kat.

"Kat..."

Tish's voice was uncertain, and hysteria was rising in her eyes. It wasn't just fear of jail. Kat recognized cold feet and the fear of damnation.

Tish was about thirty-six seconds from turning on her and damn her divorce settlement and honor among thieves.

"Kat. What's going on? Do you know what's going on?"

Kat took a breath and steadied herself.

"Do I *know* what's going on? No, I don't know, Tish," she said. Her voice didn't even shake. Much.

"I can make a pretty good guess, though. So can you, if you think about it."

Tish, dazed, looked into the now-empty safe, then turned her bewildered gaze back to Kat.

"What do you mean?" she asked.

"I *mean* it looks like Fitz is gathering up all the liquid and negotiable assets he can. I *mean* it looks like he's not planning to stay and fight you in court. I *mean* it looks like he's planning to run away with Hilary. And take everything with him."

Kat could see Tish wasn't taking it in.

"Tish. Think!" said Kat. "Where would that leave *you*? Holding the bag. An empty bag, filled with nothing but all the questions the police and the insurance company will want answers to. No money. No stones. Nothing to run the business. And nothing at all for you."

Well, thought Kat, *it isn't* not *the truth*.

Kat might not know what the truth was, but she was sure that what was in the safe, well, now in the duffel bag, was not there for an honest reason. She wasn't going to feel guilty about taking it. Much. She couldn't let Tish's cold feet send her—possibly both of them—to prison.

Tish took a sharp breath, blinked rapidly, and looked again into the safe. The color came back into her face.

"You're right," she said. "That's exactly what it looks like. That... That... That...lying thief!"

Good. Better Tish was angry than scared.

"We need a place to count this and split it up," said Kat. *And to think.*

"We'll go to my house," Tish told her. "Fitz's off with his new bimbo."

Kat flinched inwardly at the word.

"There's just one more thing," said Kat. She went back

to Fitz's desk, staggering somewhat under the weight of the duffel. She typed in the password and pulled up the security camera files.

"How do you know his password?" asked Tish.

"A four-year-old could figure out his password. It's his name."

Kat deleted all the security files and uninstalled the program. The security cameras, inside and out, went dark. Then she set the computer to back up, which would erase the files from the backup drive as well, and shut down. It wasn't perfect, but it was the best she could do.

"I never would have thought of that," said Tish, abashed.

"Now we're ready," said Kat.

They left the safe door standing open and headed down the back hall.

"What are you doing?" asked Kat sharply, when she saw Tish turn to the alarm box.

"We can't leave the store unsecured," she said.

"You want to leave Fitz a note, too? Tell him we cleaned him out, and he can find us at home?" asked Kat.

"But anyone could come in..."

"Tish," said Kat, grasping at her patience. "Someone already *did*."

Tish looked at her for a long moment before a smile slid onto her face. "You're right," she said. "Someone already did."

Neither of them bothered to lock the door as they left.

"We'll take your car," said Kat as they stepped into the night.

"Where's yours?" asked Tish.

"I was jogging, remember?" Kat told her.

That wasn't *not* the truth, either.

CHAPTER 5

THE SWAG

Kat had never been to the O'Donnell house. Three blocks from Lake Michigan, it was a large, two-story, stone-fronted place, with a three-car garage and an entire golf course of lawn around it. As they drove down the circular drive, Tish hit a button set into the roof of the Mercedes. One of the garage doors rolled up smoothly and almost silently.

Tish pulled in, killed the engine, and hit the same button. The garage door started down.

As they got out of the car, Kat glanced at the other two garage bays. One was empty. She assumed it usually housed Fitz's red Corvette. His midlife crisis toy. But the third bay...

"Oh," said Kat. "Oh."

She walked across the empty bay in a trance.

"Where are you going?" asked Tish. Kat ignored her.

She stepped up to the two-tone, pale yellow and white, 1957 Buick Roadmaster convertible like she was approaching a holy shrine.

"Oh," she said again. "I think I'm having an orgasm."

She set the duffel down on the immaculate concrete floor. Her fingers slipped gently, reverently across the paint as she moved to the front of the car. She leaned forward, stretched her arms to embrace the Buick, and laid her cheek softly on the hood. "Oh, you beauty," she whispered.

She glanced sideways up at Tish.

"I didn't know Fitz was into classic cars," she said.

"Well. Something *you* didn't know," said Tish. "It's not his. It's one of the few things in this god-forsaken house that's mine. The one thing my father left to me and not to my husband. What a joke."

Kat didn't hear her. Dreams she'd put away, but never quite forgotten, rose in her mind as fresh and bright as they'd been when new. She closed her eyes. Her fingers stroked the big car lovingly.

"Did he restore it himself?" Kat asked dreamily.

Tish snorted. "My father? No. He had 'people' for that. He said he wanted a classic car, not an old one."

"It's a beautiful job," said Kat, in the kind of soft voice usually reserved for lovers. Even the rag top was in pristine condition.

Eyes still closed, Kat didn't see the shrewd look on Tish's face. "You can have it," she said. "I'll trade you for what's in the bag."

Kat opened her eyes, gave Tish a measured look, and stood up.

"Let's go inside," was all she said.

Tish led the way through the kitchen and into the dining room, shoving aside broken china with her foot as she went. Through an archway, Kat saw broken glass and bent lamp shades on the floor near the coffee table in the living room.

"Wow!" said Kat, taking in the destruction. "You did all this?"

Tish shrugged. "I lost my temper."

"I'll bear that in mind," Kat murmured under her breath, her shoes crunching on crockery crumbs.

Tish yanked the tablecloth off the dining table and dumped it on the floor. "We can count it up here," she said.

An hour later, the two women sat in stunned silence.

"Jesus, Mary, and Joseph," said Tish. She pulled off her reading glasses (which she'd retrieved from somewhere deeper in the house) and dropped them, on their chain, to her soft bosom.

"Amen."

"I need a drink."

"Make it two," Kat told her.

Tish poured them each a small whiskey.

"Sláinte," she said.

"Na zdravi," replied Kat, lifting her glass.

When the first sip of whiskey had gotten the respectful appreciation it deserved, Tish shook her head. "What in the name of all the saints has Fitz gotten himself into?" she asked.

Kat took another sip of whiskey.

"It's...not legitimate, whatever it is," she said.

"Something criminal?" Tish's eyes flashed wide.

Silence hung between them for two minutes, five.

"Maybe not," said Kat. "Maybe he mortgaged the house and the store?" Though that begged the question: Why?

Both pairs of eyes went to the pile of cash on the table.

"No," said Tish. "I see all the bank statements. I'd have

seen the loan documents. Besides, no bank would turn over that much in cash."

"Not if he took it out with a *private* lender." Kat's tone made it clear that the kind of lender she meant wasn't approved by the Federal Reserve.

"A loan shark, you mean?" said Tish hoarsely.

Kat raised her eyebrows in acknowledgment.

Tish thought a moment. "No. Even together the store and house wouldn't bring almost a million dollars. Especially from a loan shark."

Kat didn't argue.

"You think..." said Tish into Kat's silence, "you think he was money laundering?"

"I'm not...sure..." Kat said slowly. "But I can't think what else it could be. Can you?"

Tish took another slow sip of whiskey.

"I don't know what else it could be, either," said Tish.

"Whatever it is, we need to be careful not to get dragged into it," said Kat, almost more to herself than to Tish. "Because, if that's the case, there are going to be some very...disappointed...people when they find this is missing." Kat's middle finger tap-tap-tapped on the table. She stared into the depths of the whiskey in her glass as if the answer would be revealed there.

Tish rubbed her forehead with the hand not holding the whiskey. "Holy Mary, Mother of God. How long has he been doing this, and I had no clue?"

"Probably not long."

Tish dropped her hand. "Why?" she asked, turning bewildered eyes to Kat. "Why would he do something so stupid? The business is doing fine."

Before Kat could answer, Tish made the leap.

"Hilary," she hissed.

Kat nodded reluctantly. "Like I said. It looks like he's gathering up everything he can and planning to leave with her."

"Little tart," snapped Tish and took a slug of whiskey. She appeared, for the moment, to have forgotten her suspicions of Kat's indiscretion with Fitz.

"But what about the diamonds?" asked Tish.

Kat shook her head. "I don't know. Maybe it wasn't a loan. Maybe someone paid him to buy the diamonds."

"Close to a million dollars buys a lot of diamonds," said Tish.

Kat pointed at the stone boxes that didn't belong to the store. "*That's* a lot of diamonds. So maybe Fitz *acquired* these diamonds for someone, he just hasn't given them to the buyer yet."

"I haven't seen any invoices," said Tish.

"I said 'acquired,' Tish, not bought."

Tish looked puzzled, then gave a short gasp.

"You think they're stolen."

"Let's say their sourcing is probably a bit...dubious," said Kat.

"Where could he 'acquire' almost a mill..." Tish choked to a stop. "Holy Mother Mary," she whispered. Her eyes grew large looking at the cash and diamonds.

"I don't like what you're thinking, whatever you're thi..." Kat froze. "Dear God," she whispered. "You're thinking Alfred Clapham, aren't you?"

Tish nodded slowly. "The biggest fence in the Chicago area. So the papers say."

"No, Tish. Even Fitz wouldn't be that stupid. Would he? I mean, don't the police think Clapham's responsible for those bodies they dug up in...?" Kat waved her hand as the name of the place eluded her.

Tish nodded again. "Yes to the bodies. And yes to the stupid. His name was in Fitz's day planner last week."

"*What?*" Kat's glass hit the dining table with a crack. "He had an appointment with *Alfred Clapham*?"

"It must have been. I just saw the name 'Clapham.' I assumed it was a new customer. I didn't think…"

There was complete silence as the two women contemplated what might be their very short futures.

CHAPTER 6

TISH IS MOTIVATED

Tish broke the silence. "We have to take it back," she said.

"No. We have to go. And now."

Tish blinked and looked at Kat. "What?"

The first gut-sucking drop of terror had been almost as bad as the initial drop on the Goliath roller coaster, but now Kat's mind was whirling feverishly.

She reached out and laid her hand on Tish's. "Tish. Listen. Fitz had the diamonds *and* the cash. He shouldn't have both. If someone gives him diamonds, they want the cash. If someone gives him cash, they want the diamonds. He had both, Tish. *He had both.*"

"What?" said Tish again, looking at Kat like she was three donuts short a dozen. "I don't understand why that's important."

Kat fought to keep her voice calm.

"Because Fitz was planning to take the cash *and* the diamonds. He wasn't going to give either party what they were expecting. Tish. *He was planning to stiff them both.*"

Tish's empty stare said she still didn't get it.

"Do you think Alfred Clapham and whoever gave Fitz the cash are going to like getting stiffed?"

Tish blinked rapidly.

"You're going to pack," said Kat, thinking hard. "And you're going to leave a note for Fitz."

Kat nodded to herself and looked around. She jumped up and ran to the desk in a kitchen alcove, then slapped a pad and pen on the table in front of Tish.

"You're going to tell him what you think of him, and that you'll see him in court. Threaten to sue him for everything. Tell him to go ahead and move his bimbo into the house, that she won't have long to enjoy it. You know what to say."

"Why don't we just take it back?" asked Tish, pleading. "No one has to know we were even there."

Someone would *know*, thought Kat. We *would know*.

And Kat knew, she just *knew*, that sooner or later— probably sooner—Tish would tell Fitz everything in an attempt to salvage her marriage. It wouldn't work, of course. But she would try.

And Kat would end up in prison.

Tish wouldn't be in a much better position.

"Because Tish, if we take it back and pretend this never happened, Fitz will simply take it all and disappear with Hilary. Just as he planned. It will all probably be gone by the time you open on Tuesday. When Alfred Clapham and whoever else is involved comes looking for their money and diamonds, *you* are the one they're going to find. You, Tish. *You.*"

Tish's peaches and cream complexion went white, and Kat knew she'd gotten through. Tish's eyes snapped to the contents of the safe spread out before them. Kat saw the calculation in her eyes. Sixty-five percent of what was on the table versus being buried under a building foundation.

"Suppose I do write Fitz a note," said Tish tentatively.

Kat nodded. "Make it look like you intend to fight to get everything *legally*. He'll expect that. He'll never guess what we've done."

Certainly not that we're working together, thought Kat.

Tish's eyes narrowed. "You're right. Fitz would *never* believe I'd do something like this, would he?"

That we'd *do something like this*, thought Kat. But if Tish wanted to claim responsibility...

"Our fingerprints..."

For the first time, Tish noticed Kat's still-gloved hands. "*My* fingerprints are all over the safe. Oh."

Kat nodded. "Yes. Our fingerprints are everywhere. But then, they would be, wouldn't they? We both work in the store. We are both in and out of that safe all day. But Tish, only the police care about fingerprints. If the diamonds came from Clapham, Fitz can't call the police."

"If Clapham thinks we've taken the diamonds..."

"He'll have no reason to think we've taken them, Tish! It's Fitz he'll blame. It's Fitz, he's going to be angry with."

Unless Fitz decided to point a finger at Tish and/or Kat just to turn attention away from himself. It didn't bear thinking about.

"He could kill Fitz," said Tish, wavering. "He may be a pile of dog poop, but he is the father of my children."

"Clapham won't kill him." At least Kat hoped not. She didn't want Fitz dead, either, but it would give her great satisfaction to know he'd be left standing in the middle of Lakeshore Drive in nothing but his shorts.

"He'll want his money or the diamonds back," said Kat. "Fitz probably has enough to cover the stones if he sells the house, the store, and everything left in the vault, and throws in any other money he has hidden away."

For a moment, Kat gave a brief thought to whoever had given Fitz a bag full of money in expectation of diamonds.

Whoever it was might be scarier than Clapham.

In a micro-second, Kat decided not to mention this terrifying thought to Tish, because, one, Fitz deserved to be caught between the hammer and the anvil, the shit. And two, Kat needed her thirty-five percent of the assets on the table.

"You think he has *more* money hidden away?" Tish asked, her gaze suddenly sharpening.

Kat almost rolled her eyes. Once they sold the stones— even below wholesale—they had well over a million on the table, and Tish was worried Fitz might be hiding more?

She didn't bother to answer. "He'll lose Hilary, of course," said Kat, rubbing more salt in the wound in an effort to distract Tish. "She won't stick around if he doesn't have any money." *Fitz might not even notice in the process of trying to save his neck*, she thought.

"What if he doesn't have anything hidden away?" said Tish, fearfully. "What if he can't pay them back?"

Kat was losing Tish. She was thinking of her children, of the man she'd shared a bed with for thirty-five years.

"Go pack," said Kat, hoping to move Tish off this point. "I'll wash out the glasses and put them away so it will look like you simply left."

"But Kat, what if he can't pay them?" Tears came into Tish's eyes.

Kat was scrambling for an answer to that when Tish's phone rang.

Both women froze, staring at the phone on the table like it might sit up and speak.

"It's Fitz," Tish whispered, as if he might hear her.

She was picking it up before Kat could say, "Don't...!"

"Fitz?" Tish listened. "Fitz, are you there? Why..."

Tish stopped, mouth open.

In the silence, Kat heard small distant voices from the speaker, "...like the Bahamas. Can't we go to Cancun instead, Fitzy-poo?"

Hilary's pout was audible even through the phone.

"Financially, the Bahamas would be much... better...for us..."

Kat could hear Fitz losing focus. She didn't want to imagine what would break his concentration like that, especially when he was talking about money.

"Pleeease," is what Kat thought Hilary said, but the younger woman's voice was muffled.

There was some kind of scratchy rustling. Kat wondered where the phone was and how it had been dialed.

"Could you...could you do that curly thing...with your tongue...again?" said Fitz.

Urrrgh, thought Kat.

"Cancuuun...?" crooned Hilary.

"Sure, baby, sure, just..."

Kat couldn't bear the look of grief, betrayal, and revulsion on Tish's face any longer. She lifted the phone from her unresisting hand and cut the connection. She laid the device gently on the table, then took a sip of her whiskey. Waited.

Slowly Tish's face went from white, to pink, and continued up the scale to blotchy rage red. She pressed her lips into a thin line. Her eyes narrowed. Kat would have sworn she saw a red flash in them.

Tish took a deep shaky breath, reached for her glasses, and jerked the writing pad over to her.

"Where's the pen?" she said tightly.

CHAPTER 7

THE CLOSET

Upstairs, Kat looked around Tish's gigantic master suite. "Geez Marie. Does this room have its own zip code?" she asked, as Tish grabbed a small travel case.

"Fitz's is bigger." Tish moved past Kat, through the enormous bathroom and into the walk-in closet. Kat dropped the duffel at the foot of the king-sized bed and followed.

"My living room is smaller than this," she said of the bathroom. "Do you let the Olympic swim team train in your tub?"

She heard rummaging noises in the closet, sauntered over, and stuck her head in. Tish had pulled a hinged shoe rack away from the wall, exposing a sizable wall safe.

"That's impressive," said Kat. "Does Fitz have a closet safe, too?"

"Yes, but it's empty."

"How do you know?"

"I had the combination changed when I had this one

put in." Tish punched in a combination and pulled open the safe.

"He never noticed?"

"He doesn't know it's there. The previous owner told me about it when she walked me through the house."

"You never told him," murmured Kat. *And you had the combination changed so that you'd know if he found it*, she added to herself, *because you check it to see if it's still empty.*

Tish pulled out a jewelry box the approximate dimensions of an armored truck and poured a waterfall of velvet bags, all marked with the Superior logo, into the travel case.

"Wow," said Kat. "I didn't know Fitz was so generous."

Tish snorted and locked the case. "Neither does he."

Kat lifted an eyebrow. Why would Tish rob the store when, by selling the jewelry in those bags, she could live comfortably for years?

And if Tish hadn't told Fitz about the safe in his room, and had her own hidden safe stuffed with jewelry Fitz didn't know about, what did that say about what Tish might not tell Kat?

Well, fair's fair, thought Kat. *What haven't I told Tish?* Still. She'd better keep her eyes open, because her respect for Tish's cunning was going up rapidly.

Tish pulled a large suitcase out of an inner closet. "You have a special closet just for luggage?" she asked. Tish, rummaging through the cases, didn't answer.

Kat glanced up. High shelves were lined with Styrofoam heads covered with wigs. There were variations on Tish's red, as well as blonde, brown, black, and even gray. They were short, long, curled, straight, shingled, shagged, and bobbed. "Geez. You've got more heads than the French Revolution," said Kat.

Tish barely looked up. "I used to like being someone

else once in a while. I haven't worn them in years. Here." She pushed the overnight case into Kat's hands. "Take this into the other room."

Tish followed her, hauling a suitcase large enough to hold all the equipment for an assault on Everest. She laid some folded slacks into it and went back into the closet.

Kat set the overnight case on the bench at the foot of the king-sized bed, sat down next to it, and laid her hand on the case. A moment later, her middle finger began to tap. She got up and went back into the closet. Tish, sorting through clothes on the rack, didn't notice.

When Tish came out, fifteen minutes later, her arms draped with hangered wardrobe, Kat was again sitting on the bench. Tish clumsily tossed the clothes on the bed. Layers of dry cleaner bags slithered to the ground.

"Do you need all that?" asked Kat.

"I haven't decided," Tish told her. She began sorting through the clothes, adding blouses that matched the slacks.

"Sweaters," she muttered, heading toward the closet again.

"Tish, we have to go," said Kat to Tish's back.

This time Tish was lugging a pile of sweaters and more hangers of dresses. She put more things in the suitcase. Took some things out.

"Shoes."

"*Tish...*"

"Okay, *okay,*" said Tish, heading back to the closet. "Almost done."

Kat crossed her arms and waited, finger tapping on her arm.

On Tish's fourth trip out of the closet, Kat lost patience.

"Tish, it's coming up on 4 a.m. At this rate, Fitz will have moved in with Hilary before you're ready. Let's *go!*"

"Just a minute," said Tish, wedging at least a half dozen pairs of shoes in the bag. "I'm sure I've forgotten something."

"You can't possibly…" Kat called, as Tish whirled back into the closet.

A FEW MINUTES LATER, Tish buzzed back into the bedroom, her good, cashmere and wool winter coat over one arm and another cluster of dry cleaner bags on the other. She stopped short. The slippery plastic bags slithered to the ground.

Her suitcases were gone.

So was the duffel.

So was Kat.

"Kat?"

In response, a powerful engine revved in the garage. The soft purr of the garage door going up followed.

"Kat!" shrieked Tish. Clutching the coat, she ran for the stairs.

She streaked through the kitchen just as there was a blast from a car horn. Not the tame "beep" of a German masterpiece of engineering, either. It was the boastful, loud-voiced bray of a proud icon from a Detroit assembly line.

Tish exploded into the garage to find Kat behind the wheel of the Buick.

"About time," Kat called. "Get in."

"I'm not finished packing!"

"You are if you're going with me."

Kat was serious, and Tish knew it.

"We're not taking that thing. I'll get my keys. We'll take the Mercedes."

"Everything's in the trunk," called Kat, as she released the parking brake. "You can get in or follow me. I'm not waiting any longer." She started to roll the car backward.

"No! My purse! My keys."

"Sixty seconds," shouted Kat, slowing the backward roll of the Buick. "One one thousand, two one thousand, three…"

Tish was already diving into the house. She snatched her purse from the dining table where she'd left it and spun back toward the garage. She slammed the connecting door, threw the lock, and raced to the Buick. Kat had the big car half way out of the garage door.

"…thirty six…thirty seven…thirty eight…"

Tish hurled herself into the passenger seat and hauled the heavy car door closed.

Kat accelerated backward into the driveway, hit the close button on the garage door opener, and headed out.

"You…jerk," panted Tish.

"I think 'bitch' is the word you're looking for," grinned Kat, as she pulled out of the driveway and headed downtown.

That and other words, thought Tish. "Where are you going?" she asked.

"I have a stop to make."

"What are you talking about?"

"I let you pack a bag, didn't I?"

"You were just complaining that I took too long. Now you want to pack, too?"

"Believe me. This won't take long."

Kat gave Tish a sideways glance. "Buckle up. I'm glad to see your dad had the restorers put seat belts in."

"It wasn't his idea," said Tish, pulling the shoulder harness into position. "Dad hated seat belts, but the restorers wouldn't do the work otherwise."

"Good for them," said Kat.

They drove in silence for a few minutes before Kat asked, "So. Why are you carrying a winter coat? It's almost June."

Tish looked at Kat with murder in her eyes and threw the coat in the back seat.

"Do you know how much that coat cost?"

"Do you remember how much money we have in the duffel bag?"

Tish huffed and crossed her arms, choosing not to answer.

Kat wove through the silent downtown Evanston streets and pulled up behind a nondescript gray car three blocks from the store. She got out, taking the keys with her.

"Where are you going?"

"I'll be right back," said Kat.

Tish watched Kat lift a small carry-on bag from the trunk of the gray car and carry it back to the Buick. The car shuddered slightly as Kat slammed the trunk lid down before slipping back into the driver's seat and pulling away from the curb. It hadn't taken a minute.

"That's your car," said Tish, as Kat pulled away from the curb. "You said you jogged to the store."

"I did. From the car."

Tish squinted at Kat suspiciously.

"You were already packed," she said.

Kat nodded.

"You were planning to leave."

Kat nodded again. She was always planning to leave.

"That's all you're bringing?"

"I don't need any business suits, do I?"

"What about your car?"

"It's leased. They'll find it."

"You can't just walk away."

"Why not?" asked Kat.

"They'll charge you all kinds of fees."

"They'll have to find me first."

Tish couldn't think of a good answer to that.

Kat swung around a few blocks, working her way through town.

"Where are you going now?" asked Tish.

"Chicago. That's what we talked about."

"Then you'd better turn around. You're heading north."

"No, I'm not."

"Yes, you are."

"No. I am not."

"Fine," said Tish. "Wake me when we get to Milwaukee."

She was pleased to see Kat look around, nonplussed.

"You're sure?"

Tish sighed. "How can you live here for six years and not know which way is north? Yes, I'm sure. Turn around."

Kat hesitated for another half block, then pulled into a convenient driveway and reversed. She pointed the Buick south toward the Windy City.

CHAPTER 8

THE NO-TELL MOTEL

The sky was getting light over Lake Michigan as they reached downtown Chicago.

"We can stay at the Marriott," Tish told Kat. "They know me there."

Kat rolled her eyes. "Shall we put the stay on your credit card, too?" she asked sarcastically.

Tish's cheeks warmed at Kat's tone. "Well, why shouldn't I?" she asked defensively.

"Because anyone can find you then. Don't you watch *any* crime shows?"

Tish was quiet a long time, feeling like an idiot. "This is going to take some getting used to."

Kat relented. "Yes," she said. "It is."

Tish gnawed her lip. "I never thought about this part," she said.

Kat glanced at her. "Look," she said, more kindly. "I lived in Chicago for a few years in my twenties. I'll find a nice anonymous place where they won't know either of us."

"Hotels don't let you check in until eleven."

"Sure they do. You just have to pay for the previous night. They won't say 'no' to money."

Tish was quiet again. Like erasing the security recordings, she would never have thought of paying for a night she hadn't used.

Kat pulled into a place flashing a VACANCY sign. "This looks reasonable," she said. "Hopefully, it's reasonably clean." She parked in shadow off to the side of the building.

"Pull up to the door," said Tish. "There's no one there."

"The Buick is hard to miss," said Kat, unlatching the seat belt and reaching into the back seat. When she leaned forward again, she was holding a short dark wig.

"Hey! That's mine!" said Tish. "What are you doing with my wig?" she demanded, as Kat tugged it into place over her purple hair.

"Making myself unremarkable," she said. "The fewer people who remember us, this close to Evanston, the better."

"You said Fitz wouldn't guess it was us. That he wouldn't call the police."

Kat turned in the seat and looked directly at her. "You want to bet your life?"

Tish felt a chill. She'd been scared before, but anger and the desire for revenge had overridden it. Now, just before dawn, in a car with a woman she really didn't know, with a trunk filled with more than a million dollars in gemstones, gold, and cash that had probably been the property of Evanston's leading gangster, fear was winning.

She shook her head slowly.

"Neither do I," said Kat. She pushed open the door and started to slide out.

Tish reached across and grabbed her arm.

"Wait! How will you pay for it if you can't use a credit card?"

"Cash, Tish. Cash. That old-fashioned green stuff. What we have a whole duffel bag full of."

"Do you have enough?" Tish used cards for everything. She couldn't remember when—if—she'd ever carried enough to pay for a hotel.

"For now, I have enough of what my dad used to call 'walking around money,'" said Kat. "Tomorrow—or later today—we'll figure out how to pay for day-to-day expenses. After all, we can't dive into the duffel bag for hundred dollar bills every time we need food or gas or hotels on the road. Or someone will knock us off."

Tish glanced out the side window at the lonely light in the motel office. "They don't look like the kind of place that can handle a big bill anyway."

"Believe me. They can handle a hundred easily," said Kat. "But I've got twenties. Unremarkable, remember?"

Suddenly something Kat said echoed in Tish's mind.

"What do you mean 'on the...'"

But Kat was slamming the door behind her.

"...road'?"

THOUGHTFULLY, Tish watched Kat walk to the motel office.

I should run, she thought. *Just leave her here. I can get everything back into the safe before Fitz knows it's gone. Or, go with my original plan and just take the diamonds. If I have the diamonds, Fitz might...*

No, he won't, she thought, feeling lonelier than she ever had in her life. Just having the diamonds wouldn't be enough to blackmail Fitz into giving up Hilary. *Kat's right,* she thought. *Fitz's planning to disappear. And leave me facing Clapham.*

But, she thought suddenly, there was nothing to stop her taking the car and disappearing herself.

She started to slide across the big bench seat and glanced down.

The decision had been taken from her. Kat had taken the keys.

Even though Tish quailed at the thought of running on her own, the sight of the empty ignition irked her.

Bitch, she thought, irritably, not bothering to correct herself.

Kat was back a few minutes later.

"What did you tell them?" asked Tish, as Kat got back behind the wheel.

"Nothing."

"He didn't ask? I mean, it's not even five in the morning, and he didn't wonder why we're checking in now?"

Kat released the brake and pulled the Buick around the side of the building to the rooms in the back.

"Of course not. It's a motel. They're used to people coming in when they need to. I paid for last night and tonight and gave the guy a twenty for his trouble, though I didn't have to bother. He was so wrapped up in his zombie movie he barely looked up."

"What about the registration..."

"I made it up," said Kat.

"Made it...?" said Tish, stunned.

"Sure. We're driving an '87 Civic four door with Wisconsin plates."

"But..."

"Here," said Kat as she parked, handing Tish the room

key. "Unlock the door and check the room. It looks like an okay place, but..." She shrugged.

Tish, still struggling with the concept of making up hotel registration information, got out of the car in a daze. She looked the room over, bounced half-heartedly on the beds, checked the bathroom. Nothing scuttled for the baseboards when she turned on the lights. The lock was good and there was a deadbolt. Beyond that, she was too tired and overwhelmed to care.

As she headed back to the car, Kat was coming in with her bag and the duffel. "Okay?" she asked.

Tish nodded.

"Let me know if you need help with your bag."

Stung, Tish snapped, "I don't need your help, thank you. I'm not helpless."

"I didn't think you were. It's just... Well, you'll see." She gave Tish a strange smile.

"*Well, you'll see,*" Tish mimicked Kat nastily under her breath. "Who does she think she is? My mother?"

Tish reached into the huge trunk, grabbed the handle of the oversized bag, and tugged. The suitcase didn't move.

"Stuck," she muttered.

She pulled harder. The bag moved. Slightly.

Tish set her feet and heaved. The edge of the bag came up to rest on the edge of the open trunk.

"She must have put something in here," muttered Tish. "It would be like her to try to humiliate me. Well, it's not going to work."

She took a deep breath and heaved.

Reluctantly, the suitcase came toward her. Grunting, Tish kept pulling. As the bag rose all the way out of the trunk, gravity took over. The bag tore from Tish's grasp and crashed to the ground.

"I'll get her for this," Tish panted.

She righted the bag, grateful the luggage wheels hadn't snapped off. Picking up the small, jewelry-filled travel case, Tish slammed the trunk lid, then rolled her bag into the room.

Tish expected Kat to make a comment about her flushed face as she walked in, but Kat only asked, "Which bed do you want? Close to the door or the bathroom?"

"Bathroom," said Tish.

Kat nodded.

"Did you notice if we locked the car doors?" she asked Tish.

"I didn't." *If you think you're sending me out to check, there will be blood*, thought Tish.

"I'd better make sure," said Kat. "Back in a sec."

Tish dragged her bag to the foot of the far bed, then staggered around it and collapsed against the headboard. She saw the duffel between the two beds and looked at it speculatively.

Kat came back. "All locked. God, I'm tired."

Tish watched as Kat bolted the door and checked to see that the drapes were completely closed. "Do you mind if I take the bathroom first?" She stripped off her driving gloves, lifted her small bag onto her bed and unlocked it.

Tish noticed the bandage on Kat's left hand, covered until now by the gloves.

"What did you do to your hand?"

Kat stopped and glanced down. Hesitated. Then looked at Tish, holding up the injured hand with the bandage on its palm.

"Knife slipped. Making dinner last night. Or yesterday some time," she said. "Bathroom?"

"Go ahead," Tish told her, pulling off her shoes. She

yanked the pillows out from under the bedspread, stacked them against the headboard and leaned back again. "I don't have enough energy to move."

Half true. She didn't want Kat watching when she tried to lift the suitcase onto the bed.

"Thanks." Kat snagged her cosmetic bag and pajamas from her carry on, and closed the bathroom door behind her.

Leaving Tish alone with the duffel.

Just grab the duffel, the keys, and the suitcase, she thought. *I could be gone in five minutes.*

Fear drenched her at the thought. She'd planned to be alone when she took the diamonds, but there was something...comforting...about having a partner in all this. She would have made so many mistakes already. Kat seemed to have worked out a lot of the kinks in advance.

For a moment Tish wondered about that.

Oh, for heaven's sake. Show some backbone, she urged herself. *This might be the only chance I have to take it all and get away.*

She forced herself to stand up, ready to take the initiative, before she noticed that Kat had taken her purse—and presumably the car keys—with her into the bathroom.

Tish listened to the water run for five minutes, thinking many uncharitable thoughts. She wasn't going to admit that she was relieved. She hadn't been sure she could get both her suitcase and the duffel out to the car before Kat came out of the bathroom anyway.

She sighed. Since she was up, she might as well wrestle the suitcase onto the bed.

Three minutes later, Tish was aghast, then furious.

CHAPTER 9
REGRETS AND PANIC

Kat leaned back against the closed bathroom door and shut her eyes. She locked her knees to keep from sliding to the floor. If she didn't need to sleep, she'd still be driving.

Behind the wheel of the Buick, she felt sure, powerful, in control. Only the road felt right. On the road, she was free. On the road, she was fearless. How could she have forgotten that?

Here, in this no-name motel, she was terrified by what she'd done. By the choices she'd made. By the choices facing her.

She lifted a hand to her left breast. Felt her heart flailing beneath it.

And Tish. Blessed Mary. What had she been thinking to include Tish in this?

What choice had she had? Finding Tish in front of the safe had been a shock. She'd had to change her plans on the fly. Now she'd worry constantly that Tish would freak out and turn her in.

She mustered a small smile, remembering. Who knew

Tish had it in her? That she would strike such a brazen blow when she discovered her husband was going to divorce her?

Of course, Tish had to realize Fitz would continue his lying and cheating to get almost everything—if *not* everything—in a divorce. Or she wouldn't have been opening that safe in the middle of the night.

Her smile faded.

Kat should never have trusted Fitz herself. They all knew he was a snake. He told the bench jewelers how to do their work, though he'd never lifted a torch. He preened when customers gushed over the beautiful designs Tish had salvaged from his incompetent sketches. The sales staff groused about the way he moved in to close hard-won sales they'd made. By recording the sales in his book, Fitz eliminated the need to pay anyone a bonus.

They talked more quietly about the philandering. *Certainly Tish has to know*, they said, shaking their heads, *know it and accept it.*

But what about me? Kat thought, her face burning. *Am I any better than Fitz? Didn't I screw Tish, too, by sleeping with her husband?* She'd had no idea the bastard was married at the time, but still, the knowledge always made her squirm.

Because she had deliberately used that knowledge to blackmail him into a manager's job and a promise that, first, she'd run the new store he planned to open after his father-in-law died. Second, she made him promise she could buy him out of that new store after five years.

She should never have believed him when he'd agreed.

If only she hadn't been so damned desperate.

Six years down the road, she still had nothing.

Until tonight.

In addition, by helping Tish get something from the lying worm, Kat might begin to make amends to her. And maybe find a way to forgive herself for being such an unbe-lievable fool.

I have to make her understand that our only chance of survival is to stick together. Otherwise...

Otherwise, they'd die. Clapham was unforgiving. If he ever suspected Kat and Tish had his money and diamonds...

She hoped she'd been right about Fitz being able to sell enough to pay Clapham back. Much as she despised him, she really didn't want him dead.

Kat sighed, grateful that she no longer went to confession, and set her things on the counter. Leaning on the edge of the sink, she looked in the mirror. Her eyes were ringed with exhaustion, the corners creased with fear.

She dragged off the dark wig. Her own burgundy-colored hair looked garish in the harsh light.

Stupid decisions, she thought. *They always make sense at the time.*

Yet from the moment she'd decided to take the cash from the safe, everything clicked into place, like the tumblers on the safe. She'd seen everything clearly, and she knew what she would do.

Then she'd found Tish in the store, and things had tipped sideways very fast.

Kat had only wanted the money she was owed—all the raises and bonuses she'd been promised and never been given—and something over to make up for the store that had never materialized. There was usually about $20,000 in mixed bills in a zippered pouch on the middle shelf of the safe. Fitz kept it to buy second-hand jewelry. *That* was what she'd offered to split with Tish. Kat hadn't even thought about the sapphire until the words fell out of her mouth.

Then Tish had stunned her by not only agreeing but by

being able to open the inner safe. After that, things had just...snowballed. There was no going back.

Now, here she was, with significantly more than a million in cash, gemstones, and gold that they had to sell, hide, and eventually split—with a woman who had every right to hate her, if not shoot her.

At least Thelma and Louise had been friends before they hit the road.

Kat shivered.

Jesus, Mary, and Joseph, as Tish would say, what have we gotten into?

Well, thought Kat, *only Jesus, Mary, and Joseph can get us out of it now. I hope they're up to it.*

CHAPTER 10

WIGS AND KNICKERS

Showered and dressed for bed, Kat opened the bathroom door to chaos. Tish's clothes and shoes covered every surface in the room. Fury was written all over her face. She had a silk chemise in one hand and what looked like the skin of a rat in the other.

Kat shook her head. "I was afraid the zipper wouldn't hold with all you'd stuffed into it. I didn't even hear the bang."

"Oh, you're so very funny!" spat Tish. "What the hell is this?" She shook the rat at Kat.

"When it was living?"

Tish hurled it at Kat. "My wigs! You shoved my natural hair wigs in here like they were...were..."

"Hair?"

"They have to be treated carefully! Not wadded up like T-shirts."

"Or thrown across a room?" Kat picked up the wig and handed it back. Tish almost snatched it from her hand.

"You'll want this one, too," she said, holding the dark wig out to Tish. "Unless you'll let me borrow it tomorrow?"

"Keep it," said Tish sourly. "It suits you better anyway."

Kat put the wig and her cosmetic bag into her carry-on.

"When did you put all these in my suitcase? Better yet, why did you pack them?" asked Tish. "I haven't worn most of them in years!"

"I told you. They'll help make us unremarkable. Or remarkable in the wrong way." She pointed at a bright red, highly curled and fluffed—and obviously acrylic—wig. "That one would make you look like a red-haired Dolly Parton on one of her more outrageous days," she said. "No one would remember anything else."

Tish picked up the wig and her eyes softened. "It was the first one I bought. I loved Dolly. My mother wouldn't let me wear my hair like that. This cost me a month's worth of babysitting money."

Kat smiled back. "It looks like it."

Tish chuckled a bit. "It does. I used to keep it in my girl-friend's locker. I'd put it on in the girl's bathroom and take it off before I caught the bus home." She laid the wig gently back into her bag.

Kat looked around the room at the destruction.

"What are you looking for?" she asked Tish.

"A nightgown. I forgot my stupid nightgowns."

"I can't believe you forgot anything."

"You were rushing me!"

"I wasn't rushing you. You had more than an hour."

"I needed more time."

"You were packing the whole closet!"

"I was not! I only packed the necessities."

Kat pointed at the wool coat draped over a chair. "Like that?"

"I told you. That coat cost a lot of money."

Kat pointed down to the duffel. "A lot of money."

Tish simply fumed.

"Let's talk about this in the morning," said Kat. "Or later this morning. I'm exhausted."

"I don't have a nightgown!"

"Oh, for God's sake, Tish..."

"I should have brought another suitcase."

"For nightgowns?"

"And underwear. I didn't pack my underwear!"

Kat wrinkled her brow. "I saw you put a stack of panties and bras on the bed."

"You took my suitcase before I could pack them."

Kat rubbed her forehead.

"Look. We'll shop for underwear tomorrow. Right now, I just want to sleep," she said.

"But I don't have a nightgown!"

"Tish, you could clothe half of Chicago with what you have in that bag. Pick something and sleep in it."

"That's all daywear."

"Then sleep naked!" snapped Kat. "Or wear your damned coat." She scooped up blouses, slacks and sweaters from her bed and dumped them on Tish's. "I'm going to sleep. Good night."

Kat pulled down the bedspread and sheets, crawled into bed, and flipped off the light on her side of the nightstand. She turned her back on Tish.

Angrily sorting through her clothes, Tish didn't see Kat's arm snake out, grab her purse from the floor next to her bed, and drag it under the blanket.

CHAPTER II
THE PLAN

"What?" Tish's voice unintentionally went up an octave. She'd slept in the silk chemise and yesterday's underwear. She wasn't a happy woman this morni... afternoon.

"Keep your voice down," said Kat, looking quickly at the other diners at Lou Mitchell's. They'd slept until after two, but regardless, they were ready for breakfast, and Mitchell's served breakfast all day. The car, with the duffel in the trunk, was parked outside at the curb where they could watch it from their table.

"I thought you had a plan!"

"That is my plan."

"A road trip?" hissed Tish.

"Didn't you see Thelma and Louise?"

"Yes. They drove off a cliff," said Tish. "I'm beginning to know what that feels like."

"Okay. Maybe that was a bad example. We're not going to drive off a cliff and we're not going to die."

"Oh? I think Alfred Clapham might think differently about that, don't you?"

"Tish, right now, we don't exist for Alfred Clapham. No one knows we have... what we have."

"Then why do we have to go on a road trip?"

"Because the...things...do us no good unless we can sell them."

"This is Chicago. We can sell them here."

"One pawn broker will talk to another one, and they'll ask questions, and sooner or later, one of them will be crooked and word will get back to Clapham. Then we *will* die."

Tish was quiet. Kat was right about that, at least.

"Hello, ladies!" The hearty voice of their server startled them both. "I'm Di. Coffee?" She slid two small plates holding a couple donut holes each—the Lou Mitchell's signature breakfast opener—onto the table and held up the coffee pot.

"Please," said Kat. Tish nodded.

"Are you ready to order?" Di asked while she poured.

When she'd taken their order and their menus, and was out of earshot, Kat leaned across the table.

"A road trip is something no one would think of," she said, "even if someone did somehow find out and start looking for us. Look. We go to small towns, find pawn shops, and sell the..." She looked around quickly to make sure no one was listening. Lou Mitchell's was a busy place, and there were tables close to the booth where they sat, although the noise level was high, and Tish doubted anyone could hear them. She had a hard time hearing Kat from across the table. Kat still dropped her voice. "...inventory," she finished. "If we spread them out across the country, no one will suspect."

"Across the *country*?" Tish was aghast.

"Yes."

"You're insane."

"What do *you* suggest then?" snapped Kat. She caught herself and lowered her voice. "We hang around in Chicago until we're caught?"

"I know a bunch of jewelers and stone dealers…"

"They'll buy stolen goods from you?"

Tish stopped. Kat was right. *Again.*

Of course, they couldn't sell the stones to the dealers Superior usually worked with, and that went for the jewelers Tish knew, too. Someone would almost certainly call Fitz if she tried. Even if they were interested in buying, they'd wonder why Tish was selling the stones, and they'd insist on paying by check, not cash, which they'd make out to Superior Jewelers.

Either way, she'd be busted.

Now there were also the *other* diamonds. If those *did* come from Clapham, it was more than likely they'd already been stolen. Once the news leaked that Fitz had been robbed, if Tish showed up anywhere with the fence's stones…

She'd be lucky if she only went to prison.

She hated to admit it, but to realize any money from the stones—and live to enjoy it—they had to leave the area. As anonymously as possible.

"Okay," she finally said. "Road trip. Where did you have in mind? New York?"

"Route 66," said Kat.

"What? Why?" said Tish, astonished.

"One: Because it's quiet. Two: Because it goes through small backwater towns where no one will look for us."

"Small towns where everyone is bored so mindless they won't even notice a big, old, *yellow* 1957 Buick driving down Main Street piloted by two middle-aged women who want to sell...inventory?" asked Tish, every word dripping honeyed sarcasm.

She was glad to see Kat hesitate for a moment.

"No," said Kat finally. "I don't think anyone *will* pay any particular attention to the car."

"Why not? It's big. It's ugly..."

"Because, three: The Buick's a classic. Lots of classic cars cruise the Route. People *rent* classic cars to drive the Route. They want to relive the post-war heyday of road travel." Kat looked out the window, and Tish followed her gaze. At the curb, two guys were checking out the car in question. "In fact, it's probably more anonymous to drive the Buick on Route 66 than it would be to drive it on the highway. Or in a big city."

"There's a lot more money along the east coast," said Tish. *Not to mention better food and hotels, too*, she thought. "Why not go up that way?"

"Simple. Four: Route 66 ends up in California. If you're going to end up with a...significant retirement, do you want to spend your winters in the northeast? I've heard you complaining every year about the Great Lakes' winters. For the last six years."

Tish *did* hate the winters. She'd hated them all her life. Stepping into the gray-black snow piled at the curb, half-frozen slop spilling into your shoes. Mud splashed up your calves. Nose running from the cold. The wind off the ice on Lake Michigan cutting through your clothes like you were naked—when you weren't sweating under too many layers.

She wouldn't admit it to Kat, but she'd always dreamed of going to California.

"And five: It could be fun."

"Fun? With you?"

Kat waved the comment away.

"Honestly, Tish. When was the last time you went on a vacation?"

Tish opened her mouth, but Kat wasn't finished.

"I mean an honest-to-goodness vacation, when you weren't walking up and down convention center aisles in Germany or Hong Kong? Where you weren't trying to find the best deal on jewelry, and didn't have to be anywhere at any given time? When you just followed your heart? Certainly not in the time I've worked for you."

The snide response on Tish's lips faltered.

A long-ago summer. A dirt road along the shimmering lake. A tiny cabin on a small cove. A beat-up car they weren't sure would even get them home.

And they hadn't cared.

Her summer of heartbreak.

"I don't really remember," said Tish, dragging the door to memory lane closed.

Her father had thought vacations were a waste of time. So did Fitz, unless he was off somewhere with some new love interest.

"See?" said Kat. "You owe it to yourself."

She did owe it to herself, thought Tish. She'd been cheated out of so much.

"Maybe you're right," she said slowly. "It could be fun." Then her eyes focused sharply on Kat. "But not without underwear and a nightgown."

"No problem. We have time. Fitz won't know anything is wrong until Tuesday when he opens the store. We can hit the road tomorrow."

"All right, ladies, here you go," said their server, smiling, as she placed hot plates in front of them. "Hope you're hungry. If you need anything else, just shout."

"I don't know about you," Tish told Kat, "but I'm starving."

"I could certainly eat," said Kat. "I say we just forget about...everything, at least for a little while."

That was a mistake.

CHAPTER 12

THE MORNING AFTER

A scant fifteen miles north, Fitz O'Donnell steered his lipstick-red Corvette convertible through the shady lanes of Evanston, one hand on the wheel, the other arm draped—somewhat uncomfortably—across the silky, bare shoulders of the lovely Hilary. It was a brilliant Sunday afternoon. The top was down, the sun was glittering on Lake Michigan, and Hilary's warm fingers were stroking his tanned thigh at the edge of his tennis shorts. Her acrylic nails, the same shade as the Corvette, raked along his skin with just enough pressure to keep him interested.

The lake shore would soon be clotted with barbecuers and beer drinkers for the Memorial Day celebration, but he and his lovely Hilary had other destinations in mind. Much warmer, much more relaxed destinations. Their packed bags in the trunk reflected that. Soon, winter winds laced with icy needles would be a thing of the past.

So would that damned albatross of a store. He'd wanted to get rid of it ever since old man Ryan had finally died three years ago. Every time he'd mentioned it, though, Tish had gone nuts, yammering about her birthright or inheritance or something.

Then he'd met Hilary, and everything had become clear.

Fitz smiled into the breeze. Life was looking very bright indeed. He'd had a few pangs the other night, when he'd told Tish he was leaving her, but they were forgotten now. She'd assumed he was asking for a divorce, but divorces cost money and were always messy according to his friends at the country club. So why bother? No one in the Bahamas would ask if he was really divorced. And Hilary—dear Hilary!—well, he'd just told her Tish had agreed.

Well, she would have, anyway, if she'd stopped shrieking long enough to realize the store and the house would be hers. And good riddance.

Let her file for divorce if she wanted. Her attorney would have to find him first.

Yes, happy endings all around.

He'd already forgotten Kat Merevec. Just as he'd conveniently forgotten Alfred Clapham.

Tish could deal with it. After all, she'd always wanted to run the business.

Fitz turned into the lot behind the store and stopped the engine in his usual parking space.

"Now, sweetest," he said, turning a megawatt smile of capped teeth on Hilary, "we'll just pick up our nest egg. Then Baha...I mean, Cancun beaches, here we come!"

Fitz had agreed to Cancun in a moment of passion the previous night, but after a few days, they'd be off to the Bahamas. After all, that's where there were people who could take care of converting the gold and stones into untraceable cash. More untraceable cash.

It would be a wrench to turn over the Corvette to a new

owner on the way to the airport, and Hilary would pout, but it was a small sacrifice in the greater scheme of things.

Hilary leaned in toward him, slid her fingers between his thighs, and squeezed.

"I'm sooo excited," she whispered.

Fitz almost came right there.

"There's no one in the store." He produced his best imitation seductive smile. "The couch in my office is quite... long," he said.

She wrinkled her perfect nose, and sunlight shimmered off her perfectly colored blonde hair.

"Perfect," she said.

They climbed out of the car. Fitz, twining his fingers with those of his beloved, walked awkwardly to the back door of his—soon to be former—jewelry store. Hilary was already working the fingers of her free hand into his shorts to unfasten them, as Fitz pushed the key into the lock and... the door swung open.

Fitz's junk shriveled and hid.

"Dear God," he whispered.

Hilary, aware only that she'd lost his attention, pouted. "Fitzy!"

"The door's unlocked," he said.

"You said no one was here." Her lips pooched out further.

Fitz dropped her hand, slowly pushed the door open the rest of the way, and stepped cautiously inside.

Across the room, the alarm blinked green.

Could he have forgotten to lock up the other night? Had he been that anxious to get his confrontation with Tish over and get to Hilary's condo?

Had the store been unlocked all weekend?

"Dear God," he whispered again.

It finally dawned on Hilary that something was not right.

"Fitzy. Baby, what's wrong?"

Fitz didn't answer. He was already moving to the front of the store.

Across the showroom, he saw the vault door.

Secure.

"It's okay," he said, gasping with relief. "I was afraid someone had gotten in."

"Then we're all alone after all," Hilary simpered up to him.

Fitz smiled gamely. He wasn't at all sure he was up to… anything…after having the piss almost literally frightened out of him.

Then again, he thought, looking at that perfect face and feeling her hands on him, maybe he could manage something.

He slipped his arm around her waist and tugged her toward his office. Giggling, she skipped alongside him.

"Here, it is, sweetness! Here's where I keep the big surpr…"

Fitz stopped so suddenly, Hilary, half wrapped around him, stumbled.

"What surprise, baby? Show your Hillie."

Fitz peeled her hands off him and, dazed, moved across the office. The big black safe gaped at him. Fitz's white face gaped back from the mirrored closet doors.

It can't be empty, he thought in bewilderment. *I put everything inside on Saturday.*

He blinked harder. The black void in front of him had to be a mirage. A hallucination.

Because if it wasn't…

His mouth went dry, and his scrotum took a fast trip north.

Hilary's busy hands were back inside his pants, and she was gabbling at him.

"Where's my surprise, Fitzy-poo? Hillie wants her surprise."

"Shut up," he said, shoving her hands away.

"What?" said Hilary, stunned.

He turned an angry face to her. "Shut. Up."

Her blue eyes widened in shock, then her eyebrows came down in a thunderous frown.

Fitz turned back to the safe.

"I have to think," he said.

CHAPTER 13
THE BUY IN

"Check your phone and see if there's a locker service nearby," said Kat, finishing the second of her donut holes.

"Where's *your* phone?" asked Tish. She hadn't seen or heard Kat's phone in the time they'd been together. Kat was never without it at the store.

"I left it in my car," said Kat.

"You forgot your *phone*?" Kat would as soon forget her arm, thought Tish. "You never put it down at the store. I thought it was surgically implanted."

"*You* forgot your underwear," said Kat.

"That was not my fault."

"We have to find a locker service before we can do anything," said Kat. "We can't leave..." she dropped her voice, "our inventory...in the trunk while we shop."

"We can't just hand over the duffel," protested Tish. "There's no guarantee that someone at the service won't open up the bag."

"True. As it is, it's not secure," said Kat. "So, I guess first, before the locker service and underwear, we need a luggage store. If we get a hard-sided suitcase for our inventory, it'll look just like any other bag being checked by tourists."

Tish sighed. She was getting tired of Kat being right all the time, even though she really wanted fresh underwear.

"We passed a small luggage store on the way here," Tish told her. "We can stop there on the way back. I think there was parking on the street."

Kat smiled. "You're learning."

As they ate, Tish thought about all the other things she'd "learned." Not to use a credit card. Not to give more information than necessary. To stay away from people she knew in her previous life.

And wigs...

"Kat," she said slowly.

Kat looked at her over the rim of her coffee cup.

"You said the wigs would be useful."

"Umm." Kat was noncommittal.

"Because we might want the...merchants...we present with our...inventory...to be a bit...fuzzy...about who sold it to them. Or," she went on, more confidently as Kat opened her mouth to answer, "more accurately, so that their cameras might be a bit fuzzy about the sellers."

"You *are* learning," said Kat quietly.

"So why stop with wigs?" asked Tish.

For a moment Kat looked confused. "I'm sorry?"

"I was in the theater class in high school and, before I married Fitz, I volunteered with the community theater in Evanston."

"You were onstage?" Kat was surprised.

"Oh, no. I wasn't really... That was... I couldn't do that. But I loved everything else—lighting, scenery." She looked into Kat's sapphire-blue eyes. "Costuming."

Tish hesitated.

Kat put her coffee cup down. "Go on."

Tish felt a rush of excitement. "So, if wigs are helpful, suppose we went a little further?"

Kat looked at her inquiringly.

"I got really pretty good with stage makeup," Tish went on, getting so animated she struggled to keep her voice down. "Our kids always had the best Halloween costumes." She smiled. "I'm a demon at a thrift store."

Slowly, Kat grinned back. "Well, then," she said. "Luggage, locker, undies, and greasepaint. An unusual shopping list. For an unusual team."

She lifted her coffee cup and held it out. Tish raised hers, touched it to Kat's, and to her surprise, laughed.

THEY BOUGHT TWO HARD-SIDED, silver suitcases at the luggage store. Back at the hotel, they shifted the cash, gold, and gemstones to the new, large carry-on bag. Naturally they squabbled over what combination to use, each voting for her own birthdate, until Kat suggested the date of the robbery.

"Like I want to be reminded of the date my husband of thirty-five years says he wants a divorce," said Tish.

"It's the one date both of us can remember," Kat reasoned.

"I guess that's true. I don't have a better idea. Go ahead and set it."

Before Kat closed the lid, Tish stopped her. Reaching past her partner in crime, she pulled two thousand dollars out.

"What are you doing?" asked Kat.

"Here." Tish handed Kat $500 and kept the same for herself. "For personal stuff."

"Like nightgowns?"

Tish made a face at her. "Yes. Or anything else. Like toothpaste or, I don't know, magazines or..." she said, with a wide-eyed innocent look at Kat, "...condoms."

Kat's eyes narrowed. "And the other thousand?"

"Shared...shall we call them business expenses? Hotels, food, gas..."

Kat considered. "You're right. Putting this enterprise on a business footing is a good idea. A very good idea."

Tish held out three hundred-dollar bills to Kat.

"Here. You paid for the hotel room out of your own money and bought the suitcases. From now on, everything comes out of our 'expense account.'" She pointed at the stash in the carry-on.

"Oh. No. That's okay," said Kat, not reaching for the money. "It wasn't that much..."

"I insist," said Tish. "We'll keep it square from the beginning."

"Well. All right," said Kat, taking the cash almost reluctantly. She was silent as she put the money in her purse. Over her shoulder, she said to Tish, "I think you'd better be the banker."

"Me?" Tish couldn't keep the surprise out of her voice. "You trust me to handle this?" Tish blinked.

"Of course. You took care of all the store finances." Kat snapped her purse shut. "I've seen you do math in your head, and it's always been exact, to the penny. Who better to handle our expenses on this...enterprise?"

"Oh," was all Tish had been able to say, as Kat turned away to lock the suitcase. When she turned back, Tish was simply standing there, money in hand.

"Well? Are we going shopping or what?"

"What? Oh, yes. Shopping." Tish, bemused, folded their expense money and tucked it into a separate pocket in her handbag.

"I think a locker was next on our list?" she said.

CHAPTER 14
MÉNAGE À TROIS

"Hillie isn't happy, Fitzy," said Hilary.

Like I can't see that, thought Fitz, as he paced in front of the big window overlooking the golf course. She'd been complaining since he'd dragged her from the store. Now she sat glowering on the sofa, arms and legs crossed, foot waving in the air.

"We should be in Cancun," she added. For the twenty-second time. Fitz was keeping count.

His phone buzzed in his hand. He glanced down. Thank God.

"Carlisle," he said, opening the connection.

"Hey, Pop. What's up?"

Pop. Fitz hated being called Pop. It was too close to Pops, and a short step from there to Grandpa.

"Bit of bad news," he said, trying to be nonchalant. "Stopped by the store to pick up a bit of cash," he said, "and, well, I've been robbed."

Silence.

"You're not serious," said Carlisle weakly.

"Yeah. I'm afraid I am."

"Are the police there now?"

"No. No, I'm... I haven't called the police."

There was a pause on the other end of the phone. "Why the hell not?" Carlisle finally asked. "I mean...if you've been robbed..."

"Well, that's kind of something I need to talk to you about."

"Oh?"

"But, not on the phone..."

"Oh...kay," said Carlisle, after another pause. "Sure. Yeah. I can run by the house, and we can talk."

"Ah, not the house," said Fitz.

"Not the house?"

"No. Well, you see, that's the other thing." He hadn't planned to tell his kids. At least not now, not yet.

Not until he and Hilary were in the Bahamas.

But Carlisle was a man of the world. Surely he'd understand.

"You see, well, I've kind of..." Shit. This was harder than he'd thought it would be. "Your mom and I had kind of a fight. I'm... Well, I'm with a friend."

"A friend."

"Yeah."

"What friend?"

"Just a friend! What's with the interrogation?"

"'Just a friend'?" said Hilary. The words sizzled in the air behind him.

Shit. He'd forgotten she was there.

"Who's that?" asked Carlisle.

"No on..." Fitz cut the word off as he realized who was listening. "Look, I just need to talk to you. Can't you just accept that?"

"You've left Mom, haven't you? That's why you needed the cash?"

His son sounded less understanding than he'd hoped.

Fitz massaged his head with his free hand. Crap. Was his hair thinning? He patted it back into place. He'd have to check.

"Look. I just need to talk to you. Can you come by here?" He gave Carlisle the address.

"Okay. Got it. Be there in an hour."

"An hour?"

"It's not like I don't have a life, Pop. Just because you screw yours up..."

"Okay, okay. You're right. Thanks, son," said Fitz, but Carlisle had already broken the connection.

The foursome out on the green looked like they didn't have a care in the world. A couple hours earlier, Fitz had looked like that, too.

"A friend?"

He turned.

"I'm just 'a friend'?" asked Hilary.

"No, Hillie, no honey," he gushed, moving quickly to slide in next to her on the leather couch. He put his arm around her. She cut her eyes at him. She didn't uncross her arms, but she didn't pull away, either.

"You see, I just haven't told him yet. Haven't told any of the kids. Things have happened so quickly." He bent his head to hers. "I never expected anyone as wonderful as you coming into my life." He nuzzled her neck. "I'm sure they'll be happy for both of us."

She loosened up and snuggled toward him.

"He's coming over now?" she asked.

"Ummm."

"Why?"

"Ummm?"

"I mean, why did you call him?" She giggled. "Your moustache tickles."

"Num num num," Fitz said into her neck. "Carlisle is a money guy. He'll know what to do."

"I know what to do," said Hilary, a bit sharply. "Just call your insurance company."

Fitz stopped nibbling. Thought.

Smiled.

"I will," he said, stroking Hilary's stomach, edging his hand downwards. "Later…"

Hilary started to massage his leg. "Do it now," she whispered to him."

"I'm not ready yet."

"No, silly." Hilary slapped him on the leg. It was a bit more than playful, and Fitz intent on her shorts, didn't hear the hint of irritation in her voice. "Call the insurance company *now*. Then we can get our money and get on our way to Cancun."

Our money, thought Fitz.

"As soon as we're finished here," he said, as he slipped his hand into the front of her shorts. He was gratified when she moaned a bit.

"When is Carlisle coming?" she asked, sinking her hands into his hair and her teeth into his ear.

"Not as soon as I am," Fitz murmured into her neck.

Hilary giggled.

By the time Carlisle rang the bell, Fitz had texted his insurance agent and was buttoning up his shirt. Hilary was in the shower. Still. She was using enough water to drain

Lake Michigan. No wonder the water bill—which he paid—was so high.

"Thanks for coming," he said, ushering his son in.

Carlisle looked at his father's chest disappearing behind the buttons and lifted an eyebrow. "Jesus, Pop."

"Coffee?"

"I think something stronger is called for, don't you?" asked Carlisle. "I doubt I can use what you have," he looked his father up and down, "to calm down."

"Okay, look," snapped Fitz, his glow dampening. "So I've found a little happiness later in my life. You don't have to be such a prick about it. Geez. You sound like your mother."

"Fine. So, tell me why you can't call the police about a robbery."

Fitz hesitated, glancing toward the sound of running water. "Let me get you that drink, and we'll go outside."

CARLISLE RUBBED HIS FOREHEAD. "I can't believe this. You take hot diamonds from a guy who leaves bodies around like party favors and offer to trade them for a bag of cash from a shady sheik from some cat box in the Middle East..."

"I don't know he's an Arab."

Carlisle dropped his hand and glared at his father. "You don't know who he is at all! You still thought this was a good idea *before* you decided to steal both the diamonds and the cash!"

"It would have been fine if I hadn't been robbed." He glanced fearfully back into the condo through the sliding door. Hilary had an unnerving habit of hearing what he didn't want her to hear. "Keep your voice down. Hilary doesn't know about the diamonds."

"Fine." Carlisle looked at Fitz in disbelief. "Right. It would have been fine." Carlisle shook his head and turned to gaze over the golf course. He took a long drink of the scotch. "The really pathetic thing is, I don't think you even realize how much deep shit you're in."

"Actually, Hil had a good idea."

"Oh, this ought to be good," muttered Carlisle. "She can make a cappuccino and think, too."

"Hilary is actually quite bright," said Fitz defensively. "She was underutilized."

"Sure she was."

"Maybe you should shut up and listen," shot back Fitz.

"Okay, yeah. Sure. Let's hear what the brain trust had to say." Carlisle faced his father and leaned back against the deck railing, crossing his arms and ankles. He rattled the ice in his glass ominously.

"Insurance," said Fitz, smiling. "I put in an insurance claim and get all the money back. Easy peasy."

"And when they ask for a police report and an inventory?"

Fitz's smile faded. "What?"

Carlisle sighed. "You said the back door was open. The alarm was off. The insurance company is going to want to know how the thieves got in and got through the time lock on the vault. They'll need a police report."

"Time lock?" said Fitz, his face going blank.

"Yes. The time lock on the vault."

"They didn't touch the vault. They only hit the safe."

There was a long silence while Carlisle stared dumbfounded at his father.

"You kept almost a million in cash and an equal amount in diamonds in that piece of shit in the closet?"

And the gold, thought Fitz. He hadn't told Carlisle—or Hilary—about the gold. "It's a solid safe."

"It's crap. A child could open that safe. A child did. I figured out the combination on that safe years ago."

"You couldn't have! Nobody has the combination."

"It's your birthday, Pop. Anyone could figure it out. But no one has to. Everyone knows it. Mom knows it. All the store managers know it." He lifted his chin toward the condo. "Even your 'friend' probably knows it.

She did, thought Fitz. She'd joked that it was probably either her birthdate or his.

Fitz was getting paler by the moment.

"So, you still have all the jewelry in the store and all your gemstones?"

Fitz nodded. "The jewelry is in the vault."

He still looked sick. Carlisle noticed the obvious omission.

"The jewelry is in the vault," he said, "but the high-ticket gemstones *aren't?*"

Fitz didn't have to answer. His embarrassed look was enough.

"Mother of God, Pop."

Carlisle was mid head shake when Hilary came out onto the deck. She'd taken time to use a curling iron and lots of styling mousse on her bright blond hair. Her makeup would put a cover girl to shame. A glaringly white halter top showed off a broad expanse of tanned tummy, and brilliant yellow shorts let her toned thighs and calves glow.

She saw Carlisle and stopped. Her smile, originally for Fitz, went up in wattage.

Carlisle froze.

"Mother of God," he murmured again. "She's barely older than Luke."

Fitz was moving toward Hilary, his mind no longer on the safe or the gemstones. He slid his arm around the tight, smooth skin of Hilary's waist and drew her forward.

"This is my lady, Hilary," he said proudly.

"Oooh. You're just as handsome as my Fitzy," she said, leaning forward to offer her hand to Carlisle, giving him a peep of her nipple. As she released his hand, Hilary slipped her fingers around his middle finger and tugged it. Carlisle blinked quickly.

"Carlisle and I were just talking about the robbery," Fitz said, as his phone rang. He pulled it from his pocket, glanced down, and frowned. "I should take this," he said. "It's Jed Nichols, my insurance agent."

"While you do that, I'll get your handsome son another drink." Hilary slipped away from Fitz, took Carlisle's arm, and pulled him inside.

CHAPTER 15

CREATIVE COSTUME

It was Monday morning before Kat pulled up in front of the brightly painted store front of Creative Costume and set the brake. *We should have been here yesterday*, she thought, not for the first time. But by time they'd bought the suitcases, repacked, and dropped the luggage at the locker service, it was already late in the day. Once they got to Bloomingdales, Tish's pace slowed to a crawl. Kat was sure her partner had looked at or tried on every nightgown and bra in the store. She was equally sure Tish was doing it to irritate her. The store had closed around them as Tish was putting her new bottle of Shalimar in her purse. Kat had been ready to strangle her newfound partner.

Now she looked up at the narrow, three-story building snugged in between a small, renovated apartment house and sandwich shop.

"This is it?" she asked in surprise.

"This is it," said Tish happily.

Her whole demeanor had changed. She looked younger, lovelier. Alive.

84

"Oh, my heavens, I'd forgotten how much I loved this place," said Tish, scrambling out of the car.

Kat met her on the sidewalk. "You've been here often?"

"Loads of times. I used to look for excuses to come down here when I was costuming for high school shows and then the community theater."

Her eyes focused on the store window, delight radiating from her, Tish didn't notice Kat smile softly at her, her anger from the previous day forgotten.

"Then let's have some fun," said Kat.

In the store, Tish was an entirely different woman, moving through the rooms with confidence and authority. She knew where everything was and exactly what she wanted. She pointed out the Super Mario costume that she'd copied for Luke.

"I came here to get ideas. Fitz wouldn't hear of spending this much money on a one-time Halloween costume."

"What was Carlisle dressed as?" asked Kat. "The Wolf of Wall Street?"

"Voldemort."

Kat choked, snorted, and laughed, all at once. "Seriously?"

"Yeah. Can you believe it? Never mind." Tish sighed. "I'm his mother, and even I can believe it."

"You must have had fun with that."

Tish grinned. "I made him up with the most gruesome face. He loved it."

"And Maggie?"

Tish shook her head. "No imagination. The years she wasn't a princess, she was a cheerleader. All I got to do was her eye makeup. And only until she was about nine." She sighed again. "Thank goodness for Luke. After he outgrew

Mario, he got very creative about his costumes. We used to come down here together," she added wistfully.

"Here," she said, stopping suddenly in the section of false hair.

"We have a lot of wigs," asked Kat. "Do we really need more?"

"I want to get some moustaches and eyebrows." The glint in her eye came back, and she was almost giddy as she went through the collection on display.

"I didn't know anyone could get excited about fake facial hair," said Kat. Tish looked up to see Kat's smile. "The false eyelashes I understand, but Tish...moustaches and eyebrows?"

Tish flashed her a smile in return. "You never know," was all she said, and went back to flipping through the racks of facial hair in all different combinations.

Strangely, Kat let that be enough explanation.

Next on Tish's list were putty and makeup.

"Are you going to make me up as Voldemort?" asked Kat.

"If I get a chance," said Tish.

"Excuse me?" said Kat.

Tish smiled. "Or at least change your hair color to green," she said.

"Not happening," said Kat, then paused. "Though..."

"I see you're getting into the spirit of this," said Tish, chuckling. She turned to stop a clerk. "Do you have fat suits?" she asked.

"Yes," the clerk told her and gave her directions on how to find them.

When they got there, Kat balked.

"There is no way you're getting me into that," she said.

"Hmm," said Tish, reading the product description.

"We'll take turns."

Kat stared. "Are you serious?"

Tish looked at her blankly. "Of course," she said. "Unremarkable. Remember?"

"That's pretty remarkable."

"Sure. And they'll be looking for someone who weighs 350 pounds. You wanted memorable in the wrong way, you said."

"Me and my big mouth," murmured Kat.

Tish checked out the selection of glasses but passed on them. "For the rest of them, we'll do better at a drugstore," she said. "We'll get more makeup there, too."

"More?"

Tish looked at her. "I'm in charge of costuming," she said seriously. "So yes. More."

Kat put up her hands. "Okay."

"Wow," said the clerk at check out, looking at their cart. "What are you staging?"

"My daughter's school is putting on *Our Town*," said Tish smoothly.

The clerk looked puzzled. "You need a fat suit for that?"

"For a different skit," Tish said, steadily unloading the cart.

"Oh, of course," said the clerk, ringing them out.

They carried it all out and put it into the trunk with the luggage. There was plenty of room left over.

Kat shook her head as they got back into the car.

"What?" asked Tish.

"Never again will I think you're a lousy liar," she said. "Even I believed you in there."

Tish smiled.

"Thank you," she said, pulling out her phone. "Go up here and turn right," she said. "We'll hit the CVS."

CHAPTER 16

FITZ LIES

"What do you mean the safe's not covered?" Carlisle was trying to keep his voice level, but under the table, Hilary's bare foot kept traveling up and down his calf.

Fitz stopped pacing, scrubbed hands over his face, then rubbed them together.

"Jed says they don't consider those kinds of safes secure anymore."

"Jed?" asked Carlisle.

"My insurance agent."

"Then why the hell did you keep anything in there?" Carlisle stood up from the table and away from Hilary's foot. He poured himself another drink. His third. No ice.

"Well, I couldn't put it in the vault, could I?" said Fitz defensively. "With everyone going in and out. It was only going to be in the safe overnight!" He rubbed his face again. "This is Tish's fault. She should have told me the safe wasn't insured."

He'd tried to call Tish, right after he'd disconnected from Jed. No answer.

"Mom? Why would she know?" asked Carlisle.

"It was her job to buy the insurance. She should have read the policy." Because Fitz certainly hadn't wanted to. Insurance was boring.

Carlisle groaned. "I can't believe you expected her to read the policy. That was your responsibility. It's your business, not hers."

"I can't do everything," Fitz snapped. "A good manager delegates."

"Don't worry, Fitzy. After we're married, as your manager, I'll take care of those kinds of things for you."

Both men's heads swiveled toward her, the image of Hilary reading an insurance policy almost visible above their heads.

"After our honeymoon in Cancun, of course."

Twenty-three.

Fitz squirmed. Technically he couldn't marry Hilary since he wasn't divorcing Tish. Hilary didn't know that, of course, but she kept bringing up marriage. That and the damned trip to Cancun. And her expectation of running the store when they returned.

He hadn't told her yet that they weren't coming back.

"Of course, sweetness," said Fitz, as he walked to the bar to top up his drink.

"Right," said Carlisle, turning back to his father. "So, you aren't covered for your loss."

"Well, not exactly not covered," said Fitz.

Carlisle's eyes narrowed. "What? What do you mean 'not exactly not covered'?"

Fitz took a deep breath. "I told Jed the vault had been robbed, too."

"You *what?*" Fitz might as well have said he'd volunteered to have his brain removed by aliens.

"Well, when Jed told me the safe wasn't covered, I had to think of something." Fitz was on the defensive again. "So, I told him everything had been in the vault."

Carlisle closed his eyes. Shook his head. "This just gets better," he said, rubbing his forehead with his free hand.

"My jewelry?" said Hilary, her voice knives. "You didn't tell me they took my jewelry."

"No, dearest, the jewelry is fine." He patted the air in her direction to calm her. "I just *told* them the vault had been emptied."

"How?" asked Carlisle tiredly.

"What?" asked Fitz.

"How did the thieves empty the vault?"

Fitz looked confused.

Carlisle spoke as if to a child. "Pop. You have a time lock on the vault. How did they get in?"

"Well... They cracked it the same way they cracked the safe. You said everyone knows the combination."

Carlisle's stared at his father. "You use your birthdate as the combination for the vault, too?"

"How else do you expect me to remember it?"

"Jeeesus, Pop!" Carlisle downed the last of the scotch in his glass. Looked longingly at the decanter.

"I don't see why you're acting like this is my fault," whined Fitz. "I've been robbed!"

"*We've* been robbed," said Hilary.

The men ignored her.

"Maybe because you've just engaged in insurance fraud," said Carlisle.

"What are you talking about?"

"Oh, for God's sake, Pop! You just told your insurance agent that your vault was robbed. But the *vault* wasn't opened. You lied."

Fitz looked like he'd been slapped. "Well, yes, but technically…"

"And you called your insurance agent today."

"Ye…ees…"

"The vault is on a time lock. Even if someone knew the combination, they couldn't open it. Not until Tuesday. After the holiday. Right?"

"Oh," said Fitz, his voice small.

"And you didn't call the police, first. You called the insurance agent and then me, right?"

"So? Oh."

"Yeah. Oh. How can you call the cops now when the vault hasn't been broken into? So, how will you give the insurance company a police report?"

There was a long silence.

Then Fitz murmured, "Shit."

"That's one word for it," said his son. "Now, not only can you not cover your losses—and pay the people you owe—at the very least, your insurance company will cancel your policy. At worst, they'll have you charged with fraud."

"What people you owe?" asked Hilary.

Fitz's head snapped toward her. Again, he'd forgotten she was there.

"Just some…silent business partners," he said. "Nothing for you to worry about."

Hilary pouted. "When we're married, I'm not going to let you keep things from me Fitzy. But just for now…"

Fitz sighed internally, then turned back to Carlisle who raised an eyebrow.

"Well, you're the slick money guy!" said Fitz, angrily. "Think of something."

"I manage hedge funds, Pop. I'm the guy you see if you

want to buy derivatives, not rob vaults. At least what I do is legal."

"Mostly," said Fitz.

Carlisle glared, set his glass on a side table, and went to the picture window overlooking the golf course. He scrubbed his face with his hands. "Let me think," he said wearily.

"Fitzy," said Hilary, getting up from the table and going to his side," when we're married, I'm going to be your business partner." She wrapped an arm around him and leaned in. "So, you can get rid of the others." She flicked her tongue out and licked her bottom lip.

For once, the gesture left Fitz completely unmoved.

"Pop," said Carlisle into the uncomfortable silence. "What time does the vault unlock on Tuesday?"

CHAPTER 17

THE VIRGIN'S BLESSING

"I can't believe I let you talk me into this," muttered Tish the next morning, as they motored out of Chicago proper on Ogden Boulevard. It was early, and traffic was all flowing in the other direction, toward downtown. Tish had won the argument against putting the top down, but it hadn't put her in a good mood.

She'd woken at two in the morning with demons of doubt tormenting her. Why had she thought this was a good idea?

"You were all for it yesterday," said Kat.

"I got caught up in the heat of the moment."

Kat glanced sideways at her. "You got caught up in getting even with Fitz." Then she grinned. "And you thought it would be fun. Admit it."

"You're the one who thinks this is fun," grumbled Tish.

But Kat was right. Again, though Tish wasn't going to tell her that. She *had* been mad for revenge in the small hours of Sunday morning. Blinded by the thought of it. Then, when Kat had proposed driving Route 66, it *had* sounded like fun. No, it had *been* fun, planning a road trip, thinking about costumes.

Like this was a play.

In the cold light of this Tuesday morning, though, with normal people going to work, it was crystal clear this wasn't a play. It was real.

Holy Mother of God, help me, Tish prayed to herself. She reached into her purse.

"Saturday I was a respected woman in Evanston," said Tish, almost to herself. She looked out the window, seeing her respectable past move farther away from her, as her rosary moved through her fingers. "Today, I'm a thief."

She didn't see Kat's sidelong glance.

"You were a pitied woman in Evanston."

Tish's head snapped around. "What do you mean?"

Kat's gloved hand rose an inch from the Buick's steering wheel as if to say, *Where do I start?*

"Surely you know people call him Fitz the Philanderer."

Tish felt the color drain from her face. No. She hadn't known.

"What people?" she asked, her mouth suddenly dry. She'd been sure—almost sure—that no one else knew about Fitz's...after-hours activities. She'd been able to hold her head up as long as she thought no one else knew.

Kat glanced across at her again.

"Just people, Tish," she said, as her eyes went back to the road.

You're making this up, Tish wanted to say, but the looks came back to her. All those looks she'd seen over the years. At dinner parties. Jewelry shows. Book clubs. She'd wanted to believe it was envy. Jealousy. How had plain and plump Tish Ryan caught—and kept—someone like Fitz O'Donnell?

She'd been fooling herself.

Do my kids know? she wanted to ask, but the words didn't make it past her lips.

She closed her eyes as she turned back toward the window. *Of course, they do,* she thought. *How stupid I've been. How willfully blind.*

"Ah, Cicero. We have to stop here," said Kat, making a sudden left.

"What?" asked Tish, startled out of her thoughts. "Why? What's in Cicero?"

"This was Al Capone's town. He owned the mayor, the cops. It's perfect for two molls on the run, don't you think?"

"For two thieves, you mean," said Tish. *A thief. She was a thief.*

"Well, Christ was crucified with thieves..." said Kat.

Tish looked at her in horror. "If that was a joke..." she started to say, her stomach shrinking.

"Okay, bad taste," said Kat, seeing Tish's appalled face. "But technically, Tish, we're not thieves."

"What do you mean, 'technically'? We were there in the middle of the night. We cleaned out the safe." Tish winced. She even sounded like a thief.

"Hmm. Factually correct," said Kat. "But if you leave out the facts..."

"...which I'm sure the judge will do...before he sends us to Sing Sing," said Tish, voice shaking.

"Just listen for a moment." Kat found an open spot at the curb, pulled over and stopped. She closed her eyes.

"I'm listening," said Tish, though she wanted to open the door and leave her breakfast in the gutter.

"I called you late Saturday to tell you that Fitz had fired me, completely unfairly."

"Yes, and you were distraught. We talked about this."

Kat raised an eyebrow at the "distraught," but went on.

"You asked me to meet you at the store." Kat paused, then continued slowly, and Tish knew she was thinking it through as she spoke. "You, as co-owner of Superior Jewelers, opened the safe and paid me, its recently former manager, the severance pay and bonus I had been promised by Fitz, the other co-owner of Superior, and your current, though soon-to-be-former, husband. Let us say you generously threw in a little extra so I wouldn't sue for wrongful dismissal."

Comprehension dawned on Tish. Maybe she wouldn't to go to Sing Sing. She gave Kat a long look. "I was pretty generous."

"You were. Thank you."

"What about the cash, diamonds, and gold?"

"What cash, diamonds, and gold?" asked Kat innocently. "If anyone should ask—and no one will ask—everything was as it should be when you locked the safe, set the alarm, and we left. If Fitz wants to complain about the loss of a hundred-plus random diamonds, a bag of cash, and a pile of gold, let him explain where they came from."

The rosary was still in Tish's hand, but her fingers were no longer moving.

She knew Kat was rationalizing what they'd done. She knew they were still guilty of theft. Or, at least, something like it. At least something really unethical.

But unethical wasn't illegal, was it?

She frowned. This shouldn't make her feel better, but it did.

Now *she* was rationalizing.

"Come on, Tish. Have fun," said Kat. "Let yourself be silly. No one is after us. Fitz hasn't even gotten into the store yet. He's probably still in bed with Hilary."

Tish bit her tongue. She wanted Kat to stop reminding her that her husband was divorcing her in favor of a woman thirty years younger than she was.

Still. Her breakfast was settling down to stay in her stomach.

"I thought Chicago was Capone's city," said Tish, changing the subject.

"Hmm. However, Cicero was farther away from the other gangs who wanted to kill him."

"I'm beginning to wonder how you know all these things," said Tish. "I know we ran a background check before we hired you." Tish was surprised to hear a bit of lightness in her own voice.

Kat laughed, put the car in gear and pulled away from the curb. "I love caper movies. Gangster films. Bad guys gone straight or lovable bad guys."

"So, babe, you lookin' for a connection?" asked Tish, trying to sound like a mobster. "We gonna fence the loot?"

"Actually, no," Kat grinned. "We're going to church." She made a left.

"We're *what*? Are you out of your mind?"

Kat didn't hear her. "Crap. These streets are all one way. I'm not sure... Tish, pull up a map on your phone. See if you can find St. Mary of Czestochowa."

Tish, too shocked to argue, complied.

"Chesto... Spell it."

Kat did.

"Okay. I have it."

Tish directed Kat through a maze of one-way streets lined with well-kept, two-and-a-half to three story houses with narrow front lawns and high stoops over deep basements.

"No, you missed the turn," said Tish at one point, glancing up. "Quick. Cut down this alley."

"What?"

"Turn!"

Kat turned.

And there was the church on the corner of 30th Street and the alley.

"How did you do that?" asked Kat.

Tish shrugged but smiled. "Luke calls it my superpower. I don't get lost."

Kat gave her a dubious look before carefully docking the big car in a half-full parking lot across the street from the church.

They got out of the car and stood looking up at the imposing brick building, its twin bell towers soaring like a European cathedral, each with a pointed roof gone green with verdigris.

"Please tell me we're not here to confess," whispered Tish.

"No. We most certainly are not. Come on."

"You're going in dressed like that?"

"Like what?" Kat looked down at her black slacks, shirt, jean jacket.

"You look like a burglar," Tish told her.

"Black is a fashion color. Or I could be in mourning."

"Yes, I guess you could be. Or coming out of mourning. Your hair, at least, has gone to purple."

"It's burgundy. Now come on. It looks like mass is over. Everyone is leaving. We should be able to make a quick visit."

"Why?" Tish asked, but Kat was already heading toward the door.

The priest gave them a quick look, as they moved up the

steps toward the three open doors amongst a largely Latino congregation, but he smiled a welcome. Tish smiled back, but her face felt stiff.

Kat was right. No one noticed her all-black outfit. There were enough young people coming out of the church with tattoos and piercings and hair of various colors that no one gave Kat's hair a second look, either. Tish was still glad she'd worn plain gray slacks with a white tunic.

Once inside the church, Tish halted. The space was light and airy, the roof shaped by gothic arches. High up, behind the altar on the sanctuary wall, painted medallions were more Byzantine than Illinois. Two gilded icons of the Madonna in the sanctuary increased the impression.

By time Tish remembered where she was, Kat was halfway to the sanctuary. She was startled when Kat halted by a front pew, quickly genuflected and crossed herself before sitting down.

Catholic? Kat was Catholic?

Tish did the same and slid in beside Kat who had already slipped forward to kneel, her head bowed over her hands.

This wasn't what Tish had expected.

She shot a glance at a second priest. Tish was sure he was watching them suspiciously.

I'm looking guilty, she thought. *I always look guilty. Even when I don't have anything to confess.*

And Holy Mary did she have something to confess now.

Tish knelt next to Kat and tried to pray, too, but the priest's frequent glances were making her nervous.

After a few minutes, she leaned sideways.

"How do you even know about this church?" she whispered softly to Kat.

Kat appeared to come back from a long distance and looked almost confused to see Tish.

"It was my mother's church," she murmured. "I was baptized here."

Tish hadn't been this surprised when Kat had shown up in the dark at the store.

"Why are we here?" she asked.

A tiny smile played around Kat's mouth. "Well, I'm praying, Tish. Or I was."

"For what? I don't think you can pray for God to strike Alfred Clapham dead."

"This is Mary's church. I'm asking her for her blessing," said Kat.

"Her blessing?" Tish hissed. "We have almost...we have *acquired* inventory in our trunk, and you think she's going to *bless* us?"

She shot a quick glance at the priest, hoping her voice hadn't carried.

"He's coming this way!"

"No, he isn't. Calm down," said Kat.

Kat calmly crossed herself and rose. She nudged Tish out of the pew, smiled at the priest, then surprised Tish again. Instead of leaving the church, Kat went forward, stepped up and behind the altar rail, and went into a tiny side chapel Tish hadn't even noticed. Trying to act normal, Tish followed.

Kat had her head bowed in front of a Madonna unlike any Tish had seen. It was gilded, like the icons in the sanctuary, and more like something she'd expect to find in a Greek Orthodox church, but what surprised her the most was that both Mary and the Christ child were very dark skinned. She'd heard of Black Madonnas but hadn't known there was one so close to where she lived.

Kat finished her prayer, dropped a twenty-dollar bill into the offering box, and pressed a button to light an electronic candle. She nudged Tish and tipped her head toward the offering box. Tish rummaged in her purse and added another twenty to the box. She wasn't going to be out-tithed by Kat. She made a brief prayer and lit a candle, noticing the sign by the tithe box was written in Polish as well as English.

When she turned, Kat was just rising from her genuflection and moving down the aisle toward the doors. Tish quickly paid her respects and hurried after her. She hoped the priest wouldn't say anything to her, or she'd wet her pants.

She didn't breathe until they were outside on the steps, heading toward the car.

"I can't believe you expect the Virgin Mary to bless us," she told Kat again.

"Of course, she'll bless us."

"You may be able to argue that technically we're not criminals, but I think the Holy Mother knows better."

Kat looked at her strangely. "You forget, Mary spent her whole life essentially on the run."

"You're saying the mother of Jesus was a criminal?"

"No, not a criminal, but certainly outside the law as it was viewed in that day. First, she got pregnant out of wedlock..."

"What? That's not what..."

"...and the elders weren't happy about that. Then there was Herod chasing them down. And Pilate... Can you imagine her and Joseph, sleeping rough in a stable, telling the authorities, 'No, really, sir. These three kings just *gave* us this gold, frankincense, and myrrh?' Oh, yes. Mother Mary knew all about life on the lam." Kat looked for traffic before stepping into the street, but the morning mass traffic was gone.

Shock rooted Tish to the sidewalk. She stared after Kat open mouthed, as two women, talking softly in Spanish, walked past her.

Tish blinked, and her world shifted.

Maybe Kat was right. If anyone would understand their predicament, the Virgin Mary would.

She turned and looked up at the church and crossed herself.

"Holy Mary, bless us," she said quietly. "Please forgive me. Forgive us," she added, before she turned and ran after Kat.

CHAPTER 18
ANOTHER HEIST

Carlisle was standing by the side of his wife's mini-van glaring at his watch when Fitz pulled in and parked. Carlisle yanked the Corvette's driver's side door open almost before the car stopped moving.

"Geez, Pop! We said 7:30. I've been a sitting duck for the last fifteen minutes." Then he looked past Fitz as Hilary got out of the car.

Black leather jumpsuit. Bright red lipstick and nails. Exaggerated cleavage. Usual pouty face.

Carlisle's eyes slid back to his father. "Inconspicuous," was all he said.

"If you're going to be a prick..."

"Let's just get this done," said Carlisle, heading toward the back door of Superior Jewelers.

Fitz tugged his suit vest into place and unlocked the door as Hilary minced over in three-inch stiletto-heeled boots. Carlisle looked at her and sighed.

Hilary misunderstood, put a hand on one hip, and jutted her pelvis.

"Like it?"

"Very Black Widow," said Carlisle.

She looked pleased.

Fitz stood aside and let them in as the alarm chirped franticly. Carlisle went toward the front of the store, Hilary too close behind him, while his father keyed in the passcode.

The vault was actually set to one side of the showroom in a small room behind the counters. From the showroom, customers could see the heavy steel door, but not look directly into the vault itself.

Across from the vault door sat two, double-shelved carts. Staff used them to move the covered boxes, in which the jewelry was stored each night, from the vault out to the showcases. The store was so large, it took five staff members an hour to set up each morning.

They would have less than an hour to get all the jewelry out of the safe and into Carlisle's van.

Hilary slid up next to him and pressed her breasts against his arm. Her hand cupped his ass in his tight jeans.

"Solid," she whispered.

Carlisle looked down into her face and her cleavage beyond. He felt his body responding to her scent and the warmth of her against him. An unworthy idea—yet another unworthy idea, one of many—rose in his mind.

He stepped away just as Fitz swung into the showroom.

Carlisle looked at his watch. "Three more minutes," he said, as Fitz walked up beside them. Hilary glued herself to her lover's side. Fitz draped his arm over her shoulders and stroked her arm.

"You're sure this will work?" Fitz asked.

There's no way in hell this will work, thought Carlisle. *The holes in this story are so big you could drive a fleet of Humvees through them.*

"Pop," he said, putting a hand on Fitz's shoulder, "right now, I'll be happy just to save your life."

"My life?"

"Have you forgotten," he lowered his voice, "your 'silent' partners? They won't be very silent if you don't give them what they want."

"They wouldn't kill me," said Fitz, with an uncertain joviality. "Would they?"

"Oh, don't be silly," said Hilary. "People just say that." She dropped her voice to try to sound threatening. "'Oh, I'll kill you for that.'" Her voice went back to normal. "It doesn't mean anything."

Carlisle caught Fitz's frightened eyes, then looked at his watch just as there was an almost audible *click.*

"Time," said Carlisle.

With a last doubtful look at his son, Fitz turned away from Hilary. Carlisle watched as his father punched his birthdate into the keypad next to the vault. He shook his head.

The door buzzed. Fitz pulled the handle down and out, and the vault door swung open.

"Oooh," Hilary squealed, moving into the vault behind Fitz.

Carlisle pulled a cart over to the vault door and Fitz handed him a stack of boxes. Hilary had opened a box and was trying on a ring covered with diamonds.

"Hilary," snapped Carlisle. "We have less than an hour before the staff shows up. If you don't want to go to prison, I suggest you stop shopping and start loading."

Hilary shot him a dirty look, dropped the ring back into the box, and brought it to the cart.

They filled one cart. Carlisle dragged the other one into position and quickly maneuvered the loaded cart out into the showroom, around the cases, and into the workshop. He left it by the door and hurried back to the vault.

When the second cart was by the back door, Fitz let Carlisle out to move the van into place.

"Ugh! What stinks?" Hilary put her hand to her nose and stepped back as Carlisle opened the van's loading doors. He'd pulled in so close that the doors formed a concealing barrier on either side of the store's exit.

"Marcia was hauling chicken manure for the garden," he told her.

"Smells like shit," she said.

Carlisle glanced at her, realized she wasn't making a joke, and looked at Fitz. His father had the grace to look embarrassed.

"I thought you were getting divorced," said Fitz. "She let you use the van?"

"She doesn't know I have it," said Carlisle. "If we get this done in time, she won't find out. Hand me the boxes." Fitz started passing them over, and Carlisle slid them into the back of the van.

When they'd emptied the first cart, Fitz pushed it back into the store and brought out the other one.

"Hilary can help me with that one," said Carlisle to his dad. "Go back and start refilling the other."

Fitz nodded and disappeared back into the store.

"Come on, Hilary," said Carlisle, when the woman stayed where she was just inside the store door.

"It stinks," she said.

"It stinks worse in prison," said Carlisle.

"Fitzy's right. You're a prick."

He took a deep breath. "Think of it as the smell of money. Now help me load."

Hilary frowned but handed him a stack of boxes.

They finished loading the van by 8:35. Carlisle slammed the van doors.

Fitz glanced at his watch. "I need to get Hilary home."

"I'll see she gets home, Pop," said Carlisle, exasperated. "You need to get back inside and call the police before your staff gets here."

When Fitz hesitated, Carlisle prodded. "If they find us here with the van full of jewelry, you won't be able to explain it."

"You won't either," said Fitz.

"I'm just helping my dad cheat his soon-to-be-ex-wife with his soon-to-be-second wife. I'll turn witness for the insurance company or mom's attorney."

"Fuck you," said Fitz.

"You're welcome. And make it good, Pop."

CHAPTER 19
HILARY HELPS

Fitz's morning had been hell. And somehow, as he waited for the detectives, he knew it wasn't over.

His employees had shown up just before the police got there, and he'd tried to field questions about their jobs, while he let the cops in. Of course, chatty Mrs. Fielding had to show up, just then, overhear everything, and try to force her way in, wanting her jewelry back. Fitz had to tell her it had been stolen along with everything else. (Carlisle had argued they couldn't leave the customers' repaired jewelry in the vault. It was all or nothing.) She'd started shrieking about how valuable it had been, and she'd sue. He had managed to close the door in her face and lock it.

Within the hour, the phone had started ringing with other concerned customers asking about insurance, and about how much their jewelry was covered for.

And where the hell was Tish? She should be here handling all this. He might be leaving her, but still. She had a responsibility to the store. Business, after all, was business. He'd called her cell a half dozen times but there was no answer.

"Mr. O'Donnell." One of the cops stuck her head in his office door. "The detectives are here. Can you let them in, please?"

Fitz nodded wearily and got up from behind the desk to unlock the front doors.

"Mr. O'Donnell?" asked the tall, thin, dark-skinned woman in her early forties. She pulled her badge from the side pocket of her light gray, summer weight blazer worn over a light blue blouse and a slightly flared, darker gray skirt that fell just below her knees. Her jacket sleeves were rolled up to expose a traditional analog watch on a dark brown band only slightly darker than her skin. Low heels and a short, graying afro cut longer on top accentuated her height. "I'm Detective Sam Lyons."

She held out her hand. As Fitz shook it, she nodded to the strongly built, twenty-something, Asian man with her. Dressed more casually, he wore his lightweight gray tweed sport coat over slightly faded jeans and boots. "This is Detective Adam Chung." Fitz exchanged handshakes with Chung, too.

"Is there some place we can talk," Lyons glanced out the front windows to where the local news van was parked, "a little less conspicuously?"

"My office," said Fitz.

As he turned away, there was a frantic knocking on the glass window. He automatically turned back, as did the police detectives. He immediately wished he hadn't.

It was Hilary.

Shit, he thought, and very nearly said it aloud. She was supposed to go to work. Everything should be normal.

But of course, she had to be in the center of things, he

thought with a flash of irritation.

He couldn't ignore her or there'd be hell to pay later.

"I can have an officer go out and move the reporters back," said Lyons.

Fitz tried not to sigh.

"It's okay. She's not a reporter."

He missed the look shared by the two detectives as he unlocked the door, intending to send Hilary back to work.

"Oh, Fitzy," Hilary exclaimed, as she threw herself through the small opening between the door and the jamb.

Reporters surged forward.

Fitz yanked Hilary all the way in and shut out the reporters' shouted questions.

"Oh, Fitzy. I was so worried." Hilary twined herself around him.

"My office is this way," he said to the detectives. He tried to move forward with dignity, despite Hilary clamped to his side.

Before he got three steps, Chung was asking Hilary, "Ma'am? May I ask who you are?"

"I'm Fitzy's fiancé," she said brightly. "I was so worried!" She turned her face up to Fitz's.

"It's okay, sweetie," said Fitz, mustering a sick smile and trying to peel her off. "I'm fine."

"I meant your name, Ma'am?" Chung persevered.

"Oh!" Hilary giggled. "Hilary Shoenmeyer. But not for long!" She flashed Fitz a smile.

"Mr. O'Donnell?" said Lyons. "Your office, please."

"How did you hear about the burglary, Ma'am?" Chung asked Hilary. "Did Mr. O'Donnell call you?"

"Oh, no." Hilary waved the question away. "Everyone at the Koffee Kup was talking about it. That's the coffee shop where I work. I'm a barista," she added proudly.

Chung made note in his tablet. Fitz prayed fervently that Lake Michigan would suddenly flood downtown with a tsunami. It would improve the day.

As they crossed the showroom, Lyons noticed the vault door standing open.

"That's the vault that was robbed?" she asked Fitz.

"Yes," he said, starting to sweat.

Lyons tipped her head toward the vault, and Chung peeled off to have a look. Lyons waved Fitz on toward the office.

Fitz went to sit behind his desk, gesturing to one of the chairs for Hilary. Instead, she went around and stood behind him, kneading his shoulders. Normally, this would have puddled Fitz's brain. Now he just wished she'd stop.

Lyons spotted the safe in the closet. "Was this safe burgled, too?" she asked.

"It was opened, yes, but there was nothing of value in it," said Fitz. He felt Hilary shift, and he quickly lifted a hand to his shoulder to squeeze hers. He said, slightly more loudly, "Because of its age, it's no longer considered secure, and it's not insurable." Another squeeze of Hilary's hand. "So, we don't keep much in there. Everything of value, we keep in the vault." With his free hand, he gestured toward the showroom floor.

"Mr. O'Donnell, we'll need to see your security tapes," said Detective Lyons, turning back to him from her inspection of the safe.

His heart stopped. Fitz was sure of it. Security tapes. None of them had thought about the security tapes. Everything was on there. The three of them coming in this morning, emptying the vault, loading the van.

"Security tapes?" he stalled.

"Yes, sir. Please."

"There aren't any," said Fitz, lying desperately. Why hadn't Carlisle thought of this?

"A store like this and you don't have any surveillance?" said Lyons.

"Well, of course, we do, normally," babbled Fitz. "But... But," he suddenly brightened. "We recently upgraded our security system and there was a glitch. The system crashed and we haven't had a chance to get it fixed. Holiday weekend and all."

Fitz O'Donnell, he congratulated himself, *You're brilliant!*

Lyons stared at him. Fitz tried to arrange his face to look innocent.

"How very unfortunate," said Lyons, as Chung came into the office. She looked at her partner. He shook his head.

"Not forced," said Chung. He spotted the black safe, turned a questioning glance on Lyons.

She shook her head. "Not forced either. And there are no surveillance tapes."

"No?" said Chung.

Lyons gave a small shake of her head.

"Hmm," said Chung, and turned to Fitz. "Who would have been able to open this safe, sir?" he asked. "And the vault?"

"Oh, Carlisle said anyone could open them," said Hilary, before Fitz could respond, "even me."

Christ, help me, thought Fitz, *she's going to blurt the whole thing out.*

"Why is that, ma'am? And who is Carlisle?" asked Lyons.

"The combination is my Fitzy's birthday," Hilary

blurted out, as Fitz explained, "Carlisle is my son."

"So, your staff can all open the safe and the vault?" asked Lyons.

"No," said Fitz. "Yes, the combination is my birthdate, but only a few people know that." He tried a self-deprecating chuckle. The detectives didn't smile.

"Who, exactly, has access to the safe and the vault, Mr. O'Donnell?" asked Chung, fingers hovering over his tablet.

"Well, me, of course. The store manager…"

"Store manager?" Lyons asked, turning to Chung. "Which employee is that?"

"Kat Merevec," said Chung, scrolling through his notes. "She didn't come in today."

Lyons turned back to Fitz. "Her day off?"

"Actually," said Fitz, "I let her go Saturday afternoon."

Silence hung in the air for a moment as the detectives exchanged a look.

"Do we have her contact information?" Lyons finally asked Chung, who nodded.

"So just you and your store manager have access to the safe and vault?" Lyons asked Fitz. "And Ms. Shoenmeyer. Of course," she added.

"Oh, no." Fitz's attempt at another chuckle came out as strangled throat clearing. "Hilary isn't an employee. She's a friend."

Sharp acrylic nails dug into Fitz's shoulders. "His *fiancé*," said Hilary sharply. "I'm going to manage the store from now on."

"Once the divorce is final, sweetness," said Fitz, trying to keep his voice light despite the stabbing pain in his shoulders. To Lyons, he said, "My attorney said it was best we settle that before Hilary comes here to work."

The nails dug deeper. "You didn't tell me that," said

Hilary.

"There hasn't been time, sweetness, with so much happening, and now the robbery..."

"And your wife, sir?" Chung asked with a neutral look.

Fitz's head snapped toward the younger detective.

"My wife?"

"Does she work here?" asked Chung.

"Not anymore," said Hilary, before Fitz could respond. "My Fitzy fired her, too." She kneaded his shoulders. Fitz was sure there would be punctures.

"Oh?" asked Lyons. "When was this?"

Once again, Fitz wasn't fast enough.

"Saturday night," said Hilary. "They had a big fight. Fitzy..."

"Ms. Shoenmeyer," interrupted Lyons. Her tone was sharp enough, it actually cut Hilary off.

"Yes?"

"Where you present Saturday night? At this big fight?"

Hilary hesitated. "No."

"Then please let Mr. O'Donnell answer for himself."

Chung moved across the room, pulled the chair in front of the desk to one side. "Perhaps you'd like to sit here."

It wasn't a request.

Hilary looked at Fitz. When he didn't object, she stalked around the desk and, with a pout, sat down. She crossed her legs, and her foot began to swing like the tail of an angry cat.

"Mr. O'Donnell? About Saturday night?"

I'm done for, thought Fitz. *I'm going to end up in prison. Or worse.*

He sighed.

"It wasn't a *big* fight," he said. "There was probably some shouting. I told Tish—that's my wife—that I was leaving her. She didn't take it well. Then I went to Hilary's and spent the weekend. Then this morning," he waved his hand toward the front of the store, "I came in to find I'd been robbed. Really detectives," he went on, making an effort to sound injured. "My personal life has nothing to do with this."

"Mrs. O'Donnell has the combination to the safe and vault, is that correct?" asked Lyons.

"Well, yes. Of course," said Fitz.

Chung shot Lyons a look.

"Where is your wife now?" asked Lyons.

Fitz shrugged. "I don't know. She should have been here."

Hilary uncrossed her legs and sat forward, chin jutting toward Fitz. "But you fired her!"

Fitz felt dampness on his forehead. *What the hell difference does it make where Tish is or isn't?* he thought irritably. Didn't Hilary remember that this morning they should have been on the beach in the Bahamas, or Cancun, or any goddamned place but here?

If she couldn't shut up and keep their story straight, they were all going to jail.

"Sweetie, please, let me finish with the detec..."

"But you *told* me..."

"Ms. Shoenmeyer, please?" said Lyons, slicing through Hilary's protest.

Hilary glared at her, then glared at Fitz. She sat back, crossed her arms, and began swinging her foot again.

"Where do you think she might be?" Lyons asked Fitz.

"I assume she's home." Fitz stroked his moustache. He felt sweat beading up underneath it.

"You assume?"

"Yes."

"You haven't seen her or talked to her."

"Well, no…"

"Perhaps we'd better talk to her now."

"I've tried calling, but she's not answering," said Fitz.

"You don't think that's strange?"

"Not really. She was pretty upset."

"Yet you expected her to come to work today."

Fitz looked at Lyons like she had two heads.

"Of course. It's our *business*."

"Would you call her again, please?"

"I just called a half hour ago."

"Again, please, Mr. O'Donnell?"

Fitz pulled his phone out of his pocket, scrolled through his contacts, and rang Tish. When it went to voice mail, he hung up.

"See? Not answering," he said, unable to keep the aggrieved tone out of his voice.

"But you assume she's home?" asked Lyons.

"I don't know where else she would be."

"Well. Then let's go over and talk to her," said Lyons.

"What? Now? All of us?"

"Is that a problem?" asked Lyons.

"No. I mean, it's just she doesn't know about any of this…"

"Then we'd better tell her," said Lyons.

"Fine. Well, I'm going to go back to work," said Hilary, standing up.

"No, Ms. Shoenmeyer. I think you'd better come with us, too."

"Me?"

"I have my car out back," said Fitz. "We'll meet you there."

"No, sir," said Lyons. "You'll come with *us*."

CHAPTER 20

STAGE FRIGHT

Tish fidgeted. "Why me?" she hissed, as she pretended to look at the historic Route 66 marker on the corner in downtown Joliet. Her eyes kept darting to Marker's Jewelers sitting under a gracefully curved bow window in the elegant, red-brick-faced building across the street.

After they'd left the church, Kat had made a few stops at classic Route 66 motel and restaurant signs, and wayside exhibits showcasing highway history. Tish had even begun to enjoy herself, finding interesting tidbits in *The EZ66 Guide for Travelers* Kat had picked up at a bookstore in Chicago after breakfast.

Then they'd stopped at this Route 66 marker, and Kat had spotted the jewelry store across the street. When she'd suggested that it would be the perfect place for Tish to make the first sale of their "inventory," Tish had practically started hyperventilating.

"Look at me, Tish," said Kat.

Tish shot her a quick glance before staring at the store again.

"No, *look* at me!" Kat insisted.

Tish turned back to be snared by Kat's blue stare behind the black-framed glasses.

Kat waved her hands toward herself, with her all-black outfit and her spiky purple-burgundy hair.

"Do I look like a flustered, respectable, mother of three, about to leave her husband of thirty-five years and in need of selling her diamonds discreetly for the money to do that? Am I that sympathetic woman?"

Tish dithered. "You could be."

"Don't try to spare my feelings. You know the answer. It's of course not. I'm the trashy chick at home in a pawn shop. In this place, with these stones, you are the perfect person to do this."

The night before they'd argued about which stones to sell first. Neither woman was eager to try getting rid of what were probably hot stones. That left the legitimate ones.

That, Kat now insisted, left Tish to make the first sale.

"I told you I'm not good at acting."

"You don't have to act. Stick to the truth. Mostly."

"It's the mostly that worries me. I'm not a good liar."

"You're a better liar than you give yourself credit for. What about how easily you lied to the clerk at Creative Costumes when she asked you why we were buying all that stuff?"

Tish smiled in spite of herself. "That was pretty good, wasn't it?"

"*Pretty* good?" said Kat. "That was so smooth even *I* believed you."

Tish glanced across the street, and her smile faded.

"Kat, I'm too nervous for this."

"Of course, you're nervous. You're going out on your

own after thirty-five years. You're scared. You're exhilarated. You'll be perfect."

"You're right. I know you're right." Tish took some deep breaths. "Okay. Now or never."

Kat linked her arm through Tish's. She could almost feel the other woman's heart pounding.

They crossed over to Marker's Jewelers, with the well-designed windows and the small, almost apologetic sign that said, "We buy diamonds and gold." The door pinged as they entered.

It was about a third the size of Superior, but the wood paneled cases, deep carpet, and soft lighting—except for the pinpoint spots above the cases—said 'old money buys here.' There were three people behind the counters. A young man in his late twenties and an older woman in her fifties were helping customers. A young woman was straightening the display in a case. In the corner, behind glass, an older man—the woman's husband at a guess—sat at a jewelry bench. Another young man was behind him also working at a bench.

Kat felt Tish balk. She tightened her grip. "You can do this, Mary Patrice," she said softly.

Tish gave her a brief nod and stepped forward as the young woman came toward them. Kat dropped Tish's arm. She stayed close, however.

"Good morning," the young woman said, smiling. "How can I help you?"

"Mrs..." Tish's voice caught. Kat patted her reassuringly on the arm.

Tish cleared her throat and tried again.

"Mrs. Marker, please. I'd like to speak to Mrs. Marker." Her voice came out tentative, shaky.

Perfect, thought Kat.

"Mrs. Marker is with a customer right now. Is there anything I could help with?"

Tish managed a head shake.

"Perhaps Mr. Marker?"

Tish reluctantly nodded.

It wasn't perfect. They'd agreed that Mrs. Marker might be more sympathetic to Tish's plight. But it was obvious to Kat that Tish just wanted this to be over. She was looking for a fast, "No, thanks."

The young woman went to have a short consultation with the older man who looked up through the glass.

Fear poured from Tish in palpable waves.

"You're doing fine, Mary Patrice," said Kat quietly. Anyone overhearing would simply think she was a supportive and calming friend.

Which I guess I am, thought Kat.

"Todd Marker," said the gentleman when he reached the counter. Up close he had a kind, but shrewd face overwhelmed by fierce eyebrows. He offered his hand to Tish. His fingers were long and neat and surprisingly clean considering the bench work.

"Mary Patrice Geraghty." Tish had chosen an old family name to use as her pseudonym.

"Mrs. Geraghty." Old-fashioned courtesy, not using her first name. "How can I help?"

Tish began to nervously tell the tale they'd devised. Kat noticed that Mrs. Marker's customer had finished and was leaving the store. Head bent, Mrs. Marker was listening to the younger saleswoman who appeared to be telling her about Tish's request to speak to her. She nodded, looked in their direction, and came over.

Not good, thought Kat. Two together might be more than Tish could handle.

"...so I was hoping you'd look at some diamonds I have..." Tish was saying, as Mrs. Marker stepped to her husband's side.

"We'd be happy to," said Mr. Marker. He turned to acknowledge his wife and touched her shoulder. "Monica here is our gemologist. She can take a look at them for you."

Kat caught a glimpse of Tish's frightened eyes as her nerve failed her.

With a strangled, "I can't do this," to Kat, she bolted for the door.

Her heart wheezing, Kat turned to the couple. "I'm sorry. This is very hard for her." She paused. She saw the look on Mrs. Marker's face and took a chance. "I know she told you she was getting a divorce. The truth is," Kat took a breath, like a friend about to reveal a friend's secret, "she needs the money to leave her husband. He's... Well, he's not a nice person. She's tried to leave before, but he controls their money. I'm sorry," she said, waving her hands. "More than you want to know, I'm sure. I just wanted you to understand her actions."

"And you are?"

"Katherine Miller. I'm Mary Patrice's cousin. I came along so she'd have someone to lean on. Thank you for listening. I'd better check on her." Kat turned to leave.

"Ms. Miller," said Mrs. Marker, and Kat stopped.

"If your cousin changes her mind, bring her back."

"Thank you," said Kat, and walked calmly, and a bit guiltily, out of the store.

Tish was across the street, pacing back and forth.

"I'm sorry, Kat. I'm really sorry. I just couldn't..." Tears puddled in Tish's eyes and her face was blotched.

Kat put a hand on her arm. "Hey. Come on. It's okay. I

know it was hard. But you tried. I shouldn't have pushed you."

She didn't tell Tish she felt rotten for lying to such nice people, even though they weren't selling hot diamonds.

Except, she thought, *we are*.

She pointed. "Let's go over to that little café and have some coffee. We can probably both use it."

Tish nodded. "Thanks," she said. "I know I really could."

As they re-crossed the street, Tish asked, "Did they think I was a total idiot?"

Kat shook her head. "No. I stuck to the story," she said. "They were very kind about it."

They got coffee and scones and went back outside to sit at the tables shaded by trees near the curb. Tish didn't notice Mrs. Marker peek at them from the windows of the store. Kat didn't mention it.

"I hope you're going to be better at this than I am," said Tish bitterly. Her coffee vibrated in her hand. "I'm going to be useless."

"Tish, let's not talk about this here." There weren't many people on the street, but still, they didn't need to be overheard.

"Yes. Right. Of course," said Tish, coming to her senses and looking around. "Sorry."

They sat quietly for a moment in the flickering shade, sipping coffee, pulling pieces from their scones. It was early enough in the summer that the leaves still had that fresh, exuberant yellow-green color, and while it was a bit humid, it wasn't oppressive.

"It's nice, isn't it? Joliet," said Kat finally, trying to distract Tish, who was still shaking. "I've never been here before. Have you?"

Tish shook her head. "Well, yes," she said, contradicting the head shake. "But not for years and years. A friend and I came down here to watch the filming of *The Blues Brothers* not long after I got married."

"Did you see anyone famous?"

Tish shook her head again. "No. Just a lot of crew and lights and trailers. We got bored and went to a movie." She tipped her head to the side. "Down the street at the Rialto." Tish chuckled, remembering.

Kat smiled in return.

Tish's phone rang.

Kat stiffened, thinking it might be Fitz again. He'd been calling all morning. *What if he wants her back?* she thought. *Worse, what if she decides to go back?* In her current state of mind, that was entirely possible.

Tish frowned, sighed, then answered. "Maggie. Always good to hear from you," she said drily.

"Mother, how *could* you!" came the shriek from the phone.

CHAPTER 21

HIGHER AND DEEPER

Detective Chung gave a long, low whistle when Fitz opened the front door to the house. Glass crunched as they stepped inside. Chung looked at Fitz. "Not a big fight, you said?"

Why didn't she clean this up? thought Fitz furiously. *Can't she do anything right? What are these cops going to think?*

"Well, she was upset," he said, trying to make light of it. "Tish!" he called and started to walk into the house.

Detective Lyons held out an arm to block his passage. "Sir. Wait here, please," she said.

"She's probably just upstairs..."

Lyons pointed at the sofa, through the arch to the right. "Please sit down, sir." She nodded to Chung, who headed toward the stairs.

"Really, Detective. Just let me go upstairs..."

"Please, Mr. O'Donnell. Ms. Shoenmeyer." Lyons pointed again.

They sat down.

Hilary leaned into Fitz. "We have to get rid of this furniture," she said, and wrinkled her nose. "And that ugly painting." She pointed to the landscape over the fireplace that his son Luke had painted. She looked around a bit more. "Pretty much everything," she said. She squeezed his arm. "It's going to be so much fun, Fitzy, decorating our little home."

Fitz realized Lyons was listening.

"Tell me about the fight with your wife," said Lyons, and sat down on the chair opposite the sofa, pulling out an old-fashioned notepad and pen.

"It wasn't a fight," Fitz insisted. "I just explained that I didn't love her anymore, and that I wanted to start a new life with my Hilary." He smiled at the young woman next to him. She beamed back. "Then she started screaming and throwing things. So, I left until she could calm down."

"That's all you said," said Lyons.

"Of course," said Fitz.

Of course, it wasn't all he'd said. He'd told her he'd never loved her, that he'd only married her because her father had promised him the store. Now that her father was dead, he didn't owe her anything anymore. He'd told her he wanted her out of the house by the end of the week, because he planned to start over with the love of his life, and he wasn't about to let Tish stand in his way.

But, he'd added, that didn't mean Tish had to quit working at the store. They were adults, after all, and business was business.

That was when the screaming and throwing had started.

Chung came into the living room through the arch leading into the dining room and, beyond, to the kitchen.

"Looks like she's gone," he said. "The safe in the closet has been emptied."

"Safe?" asked Fitz. "What safe?"

"There're clothes all over the place," Chung continued. "Drawers half open. Kitchen's in the same kind of mess as the hall."

"No sign of Mrs. O'Donnell?" asked Lyons.

"What *safe*?" repeated Fitz.

Chung shook his head. "Nope, but no blood, no sign of a physical fight."

"Blood!" Fitz shot to his feet, almost knocking Hilary off the couch. "Of course, there's no blood! I never touched her! *She* was yelling. *She* was the one who threw things." He waved a hand toward the rest of the house. "If there was any blood, it would be mine!"

Chung and Lyons ignored him. "Found this on the table in the dining room," said Chung and handed Lyons a sheet of paper.

Lyons skimmed it, then read it aloud.

"'Fitz,'" read Lyons, "'you despicable snake. If you think I won't fight you, you are so wrong. I will make you spend every single dime on lawyers and spend every day for the next ten years in court. When I'm done, you'll be on a street corner in a thrift store overcoat with a can in your hand begging for handouts. Where will your little tart be then?

"'So go head and move your tramp in. May you both enjoy it. May you both burn in hell.

"'You'll hear from my lawyers.'"

"No signature," said Lyons, unnecessarily.

Fitz stared with his mouth open.

Hilary pinched his thigh, hard.

"Fitzy! Say something. You can't let them talk about me that way."

"You thinking what I'm thinking?" Lyons asked Chung.

"Ummm," was the response.

Lyons looked at Hilary. "You said everyone knew the combination to the vault?"

"Well, that's what Carlisle said," said Hilary.

"I think we need to talk to Carlisle," said Lyons.

"If you want to talk to me, I'm right here," said Carlisle, as he walked in. "What's going on?"

Lyons turned toward him smoothly. "You're the son?" she asked.

"I'm the son," replied Carlisle.

"Your arrival is quite convenient, isn't it?"

"Not really. My father texted me that you arrested him."

"He has not been arrested," said Lyons, leaving the unspoken word "yet" hanging in the air.

"So, Mr. O'Donnell, is Ms. Shoenmeyer right? Anyone could have opened the vault?"

"Well, certainly my father. My mother. Probably the store manager."

"And you," said Hilary. "You said you opened it when you were a kid."

Carlisle looked at her blankly.

"The old safe, not the vault. The one in the office. Dad never kept anything in the safe because it wasn't insured. Nothing of value has been kept in there since my grandfather's day." He looked at his dad.

Hilary opened her mouth. Fitz took the hand still resting on his thigh and squeezed.

"Ow," she said, glaring up at Fitz.

Lyons looked between the two of them before turning back to Carlisle.

"When was the last time you talked to your mother?" asked Lyons.

"My mother? I couldn't tell you," said Carlisle. "I don't enjoy my mother's conversation."

"Of course not," said Lyons. She glanced at Chung who raised his eyebrows.

"Well," said Lyons, standing up, "unless our forensic people find any fingerprints on the safe or vault that shouldn't be there, or any sign that the door was forced or the alarm manipulated, I'd say what we have here is a divorce dispute. That makes this is a family matter, not a criminal one. We'll keep this," she held up Tish's note. "I'd like your wife's cell number, please, before we go."

"Are you saying my *wife* broke into the vault?" asked Fitz, astonished.

"Oh, I don't know who emptied your vault, Mr. O'Donnell. But I don't think it was an outsider. And just to be sure that Mrs. O'Donnell is all right, I'd like to be able to check on her. Her phone number?"

Lyons waited.

"All right?" Fitz asked Lyons. He was having trouble following the conversation.

"Yes, Mr. O'Donnell." Lyons glanced at chaos around her. "All right."

Fitz's face went blank as his blood chilled. They thought he'd...hurt...Tish? Maybe...killed her?

Slowly he folded down onto the sofa again.

"Mr. O'Donnell?"

"Pop?" urged Carlisle.

Fitz finally pulled his attention back into the room, took out his phone, scrolled through his contacts, and read off Tish's number.

Chung entered it into his own phone and moved into the dining room to call Tish.

The front door flew open. "Daddy?" called Madison. "Dadd..." Her feet crunched the glass at the same moment she saw the detectives. "What the hell? Who are you?" Then she spotted her brother. "Carlisle? What are you doing here? What's going on?"

"Shit," said Fitz.

Madison's head swiveled toward his voice like a tank gun, and she marched into the living room.

"Daddy. I've been calling and texting all day. Why didn't you get back to me? Why is the store all locked up? I told you it was an emergency."

"Maggie... Madison. Honey. This isn't a good time..."

Madison barged on as if there was no one else in the room. "If I don't pay my American Express by the end of the day, they're going to freeze my card! It's just $20,000, but Teddy won't give it to me." She narrowed her eyes. "He claims," she said, rolling her eyes and tossing her head, "that he doesn't have the money. Stingy pig. I know you must have at least that much in the safe in the office. Maybe more? I know Teddy will pay you back."

In the silence, Chung's voice was abnormally loud.

"Mrs. O'Donnell, this is Detective Adam Chung from the Evanston Police Department. Would you please call me back?"

They all waited while Chung read his number off and ended the call.

Madison turned back to Fitz and finally noticed Hilary sitting hip to hip by her father, her hand in Fitz's.

"Who are you?" she asked contemptuously.

Lyons had a more pressing question. "I thought you said nothing of value was kept in the safe," she said to Carlisle.

"I'm Fitzy's fiancé," Hilary told Madison and giggled. "As soon as they're divorced, I guess I'll be your stepmother."

Carlisle shrugged. "There wasn't, as far as I knew," he told Lyons.

The two younger women continued to eye each other.

"I don't think so," said Madison coldly and turned back to Fitz.

"Daddy. I have to pay for this now. They're threatening to cut off my credit. I need my gold card. I have my spa weekend coming up.

Fitz was frozen, but he felt like he was in hell.

Chung came back into the living room. "We about done here?"

Lyons nodded.

"But I've been robbed!" said Fitz, dropping Hilary's hand and standing up again.

"Robbed? What do you mean, robbed?" shrieked Madison. Then she gasped. "Oh my God!" She ran out of the room and up the stairs.

The detectives moved toward the front door.

"What about the police report for my insurance?" demanded Fitz.

Lyons turned. "If we find any evidence of forced entry or that an outsider opened the vault—and the safe," she looked between Carlisle and Fitz, "or if we can't reach Mrs. O'Donnell, we'll be back in touch. For now, this looks like a family issue."

"Or attempted insurance fraud," muttered Chung as he opened the front door.

"Good evening," said Lyons, walking out. Chung followed, closing the door behind them.

There was silence as the detectives' footsteps faded outside.

"That went well," said Carlisle. "And thank you, Hilary, for making them suspicious of me."

Madison charged down the stairs. "Daddy! My jewelry is gone! We've been robbed!"

CHAPTER 22

TISH'S SHOW

"How could you just...just *walk out* on Daddy? Desert him in his darkest hour of need!" Madison raved. "After everything he's done for you?"

Tish yanked the phone away from her ear, then brought it as close as she could and avoid being deafened. Kat could still hear every word. She watched Tish go from pale to enraged.

"Excuse me? After everything *he's* done for *me*?" Tish's voice vibrated with anger.

"He gave you a big house. *And* jewelry. *And* a Mercedes. He takes you all over the world. And what do you do? Nothing. You'd have nothing without him. Now when we need you, you run away."

"Why do you need *me*, Maggie?" Tish asked sweetly. "I don't do anything, remember?"

"We've been robbed!"

"You and Teddy?"

"Don't be stupid. Daddy! Daddy's been robbed. Everything at the store is gone. Even that money he keeps in the safe. Just when I need it. Teddy's going to let them take my credit cards away!"

Kat kept her breathing even, though her ears buzzed as all the blood drained from her head.

"Oh. So, it's not your father's 'darkest hour of need.' It's yours," said Tish.

Kat heard Maggie suck in a breath.

"Oh, you *are* hateful. No wonder Daddy got a new girl-friend. Did you know that? And she's younger and prettier and *way* thinner than you are."

Tears came to Tish's eyes. Tears of sadness or anger, Kat didn't know.

"He had the first one before you were born, Maggie," said Tish, her voice tired and sad. "I've known about them all."

Kat felt sick. Did that mean Tish knew about her, too? She'd implied as much, back in the store, in the dark. But her fling with Fitz had happened before Kat knew he was married, before she went to work at the store. Had Tish known all along?

She could hardly ask now.

There was silence on the phone.

"*Madison*, Mother. I've told you dozens of times. I want to be called *Madison*."

"I don't care what you call yourself..."

"And I want my jewelry back."

"What?" asked Tish.

"I want it back. All that jewelry you stole."

"Stole?" Tish put her hand on her heart, as if she wanted to be sure it was still beating.

Kat didn't have to put a hand on hers. She knew it had stopped.

"You thought I didn't know, didn't you? About all that

jewelry you had Baruch making on the sly. About your little hidey hole in the closet."

"I did not steal..." Tish managed to say.

"Then why did you make him keep it a secret? Justin told me all about it, you know. Just before you fired him. You knew he liked me. You've always been jealous of men that like me."

"I have no idea..."

"I want it back. All that jewelry from the safe. It's mine. Daddy said it should be mine. Then I'll sell it. And you'll have *nothing*." The vitriol in Madison's voice took Kat's breath away.

Tish was in a state of shock. Her hand was shaking so hard, she almost lost her grip on the phone.

"I will not give either of you anything," she said finally. "You can both. Go. To. Hell."

"Carlisle is right," said Madison. "You're an ungrateful *bitch*. I hat..."

Tish stabbed the disconnect button so hard, Kat was surprised the phone didn't shatter.

Kat was stunned speechless. She'd known—everyone had known—that the O'Donnell's two older kids were insufferably selfish and spoiled, but this...

Tish shot to her feet and began to pace, her throat working with unsaid words. Kat caught a glimpse of Mrs. Marker's worried face again at the window.

Great. Well, once Tish had calmed a bit, they'd go on down the highway to...

Tish spun on her heel and marched back down the sidewalk toward the Markers' store.

"Tish? *Tish?*" Kat scrambled to catch up.

She was right behind Tish when she went through the jewelry store door.

The young man was still working with his customer. Mrs. Marker and her husband were waiting for Tish, although they tried to act like they weren't.

"Mrs. Geraghty," said Mrs. Marker, coming toward them. "Are you all right?"

"I will never be spoken to like that again," said Tish quietly, though her voice was tight with fury and her face was blotched with red.

To Kat's utter shock, she wrenched off her wedding and engagement rings and laid them on the counter. This wasn't in their script.

"I would like to sell these diamonds to you," said Tish, "and I would appreciate it if you could give me as much as you can for them. I can assure you that they are very high quality. I chose them myself. I would like you to remove them and replace them with cubic zirconias. I don't, as yet, want my husband to know what I've done."

It was just as well that Kat had no role to play here because words had failed her. She had never heard Tish speak with such firm authority backed with the anger of decades.

And the woman says she can't act, thought Kat.

Maybe, for the first time in her life, Tish wasn't acting.

"We can certainly do that for you, Mrs. Geraghty," said Mr. Marker. "I should be able to have the rings for you by Friday." He reached for the rings.

Tish laid her hand gently on them.

"Mr. Marker. I'm afraid you don't understand. My husband is a vile, abusive man. I intend to leave him well before Friday. It's more than my life is worth not to. Katherine," she nodded to Kat, "has tried to tell me that for years. But it has just now been made abundantly clear. So, if you cannot do this for me now, while I wait, I will have to go elsewhere."

Kat saw the horrified look on Mrs. Marker's face.

"I'm afraid I must ask for one other thing," said Tish. "I must ask for cash. I know that is probably highly unusual. But my husband controls our bank account. I have no way of cashing a check without him knowing."

Mr. Marker hesitated.

Mrs. Marker placed a hand on his arm. "Todd, maybe we should discuss this?" The hand tugged the arm slightly.

"Certainly," he said. "Mrs. Geraghty, if you'll wait just a moment?"

As they moved away, Tish closed her hand over the rings. Her knuckles went white.

Kat gently laid a hand on Tish's rigid back but said nothing. This show was now entirely Tish's.

The Markers stepped behind the glass partition between the showroom and the workshop. Heads bent together, they were in feverish conversation. Finally, Mrs. Marker came out.

"Mrs. Geraghty. If you'll let me clean the rings and examine the stones? If they are of the quality we sell, we'll be happy to help you out."

Tish released the rings into Mrs. Marker's hand. Kat could see the marks where they'd bitten into Tish's palm.

"With a store as fine as this," said Tish, "I'm sure you have clients who would willingly buy stones of this quality tomorrow, if not this afternoon."

Mrs. Marker simply smiled and took the rings into the workshop. Faintly, Kat heard the buzz of the ultrasonic cleaner.

"Would you like to sit down?" she asked Tish quietly.

Tish shook her head. "No."
Kat didn't speak again.

CHAPTER 23

DIAMONDS AND SYMPATHY

The jewelry store was quiet except for some unobtrusive, generic music playing in the background. The young salesman had finished, and his customer had left. He was quietly working at a computer, but he occasionally shot looks at Tish and Kat.

Kat had begun to sweat as she had watched the Markers' tense conversation in the workshop. Now, as they waited, she wondered if Tish had made a mistake.

They'd planned to offer the Markers just a few diamonds from Superior Jewelers' own supply. They wanted their story of a woman, anxious to leave her husband, to be believable. Tish was supposed to show them high-quality stones of several sizes, the kind of leftover collection a woman might have amassed during thirty-five years of pulling diamonds from one piece of jewelry to set in another. They also wanted to be sure that a jewelry store would have enough cash on hand to pay for them.

Tish's rings had upped the ante. Her engagement ring held three one-carat diamonds, and the wedding band was set with four one-quarter carat diamonds. Four carats total.

If Tish said they were high quality, they were *very* high quality. It might be more than the Markers could afford.

Kat hoped not. She wasn't sure she could go through this again, and she was certain Tish couldn't.

Ten minutes later, the Markers were back.

"The stones are, indeed, very high quality," said Mr. Marker, awe in his voice. "Even the quarter carats in the wedding band. I believe we can be fairly generous." He named a price.

It was low. Mrs. Marker's eyes flickered in a wince. Kat suspected she'd wanted to offer more.

"Mr. Marker. I understand your dilemma," said Tish calmly. "That would have been a generous offer thirty-five years ago when these stones were purchased. I think a better offer would be..." Tish named a price that was about three-quarters of the retail price for the stones.

Mr. Marker picked up the rings, put a loupe to his eye, and examined the stones again.

Kat knew it was for show. Mrs. Marker had gone over them very carefully with the microscope in the back. They both knew what they had.

Almost out of sight behind the counter, Kat saw Mrs. Marker prod her husband gently with a finger. His ferocious eyebrows flashed a frown that was gone instantly. He was being outmaneuvered, and he knew it.

"Perhaps we could meet midway," he said, naming another price.

Tish thought for a moment, then nodded. "I will agree to that. If you'll include the removal of the stones and the resetting of CZs at no cost to me."

Mr. Marker's eyes darted to his wife. Hers widened slightly, meaning, *just agree.*

"Of course," he said smoothly to Tish. "It will take

about an hour. If you'd care to be seated?" He gestured to the chairs in a small waiting area nearby.

"Thank you," said Tish.

"Would you like some coffee?" asked Mrs. Marker, as her husband returned to his bench.

Tish produced a weak smile. "Thank you, but I don't think I could drink it. I'll just sit down, if you don't mind."

"Of course."

The next hour was the longest of Kat's life. A piece of steel stressed to breaking would have been more relaxed than she was, and she was sure Tish felt the same. They didn't exchange a word during the whole time they waited.

Kat had a brief moment of terror when she saw Mrs. Marker make a call. Then the woman smiled, and said, "Wonderful. We'll see you tomorrow."

Tish was right, thought Kat. *They've already sold the stones. Or at least some of them.* Kat was willing to bet they'd get enough money from that first sale that the remaining sales would be a bonus.

She felt two muscles relax.

Then Mrs. Marker made another short call, which Kat could not overhear. When she was finished, she spoke to her husband, and left the store with her purse.

Kat's two muscles tensed again.

Twenty minutes later, Mrs. Marker came back, gave Kat a short nod and a small smile, and went back to the store's office.

Another twenty minutes passed, agonizingly slowly.

Finally, Mrs. Marker came to the counter smiling. Tish and Kat went to meet her. Mrs. Marker handed Tish her rings.

"I just need you to fill out this paperwork," she said, handing Tish a clipboard.

Tish took the pen and clipboard. Kat began to sweat again.

If they were going to ask for identification, this is where they would do it. Tish had chosen an old family name so that if asked, she could tell the truth—mostly. They could only hope that the jewelers wouldn't recognize the O'Donnell name on her driver's license.

Tish calmly filled out the form, gave one of Kat's old addresses in Chicago, and her own driver's license number. She might be able to explain a different name and address, but not a falsified license number.

But Mrs. Marker didn't ask for ID.

Monica Marker, Kat realized, was trusting her instincts, believing Tish's story, believing the rings weren't stolen, but were lawfully Tish's.

The Markers had to be aware—as they were at Superior Jewelers—that the US Patriot Act required them to get identification for transactions of this amount. If Mrs. Marker didn't ask, then she suspected that Mary Patrice wasn't telling her all the truth, and she was being willfully ignorant. She also knew that, for the quality of the stones the Markers were getting, they were paying a fair price, and they already had a buyer for at least some of them. So, she and her husband were bending the rules.

Kat and Tish were home free.

Though Kat wagered there would be a strongly worded discussion between the Markers at home later that night.

When Tish handed her the paperwork, Mrs. Marker handed her an envelope.

"Thank you," said Tish solemnly, tucking the envelope in her purse. "I can't tell you how much I appreciate this."

Mrs. Marker placed her hand over Tish's.

"It's not my business, Mrs. Geraghty. I know that. But you're doing the right thing."

She squeezed Tish's hand.

Kat saw the tears fill Tish's eyes.

Time to go.

"Thank you, Mrs. Marker. I'll see that she's safe," said Kat. She gently tugged Tish's arm and steered her toward the door.

She kept her arm in Tish's as they crossed the street and went down a block to where they'd parked at the curb. Tish seemed in a daze as she got into the car.

The only time she spoke was when Kat pulled to the right to turn onto IL 53.

"Left," was all she said.

Kat obediently moved the other way. She felt like she had a pipe bomb in the sat next to her.

They rolled south, out of Joliet, quickly moving from small city to country and farms.

When she saw the Abraham Lincoln National Cemetery come up, she turned into the entrance. They had to talk or one of them would blow up.

Slowly, as they wound through the enormous memorial park, Tish began to realize where they were. She turned sideways, and Kat saw her look of disbelief.

"Sightseeing? You're sightseeing? *Now?*"

Kat pulled over. Got out of the car. Walked onto the grass and sat under a tree.

Waited for the explosion.

CHAPTER 24

THE MELTDOWN

Tish threw open the car door and stalked over to her.

"Why are we stopping?" Tish walked up and down the grass. "I can't believe you talked me into this. I must have been insane. Stealing. Lying. I can't believe you got me into this. How could you..."

Kat sat quietly, watched her pace, and let her rant.

Finally, the tears came, and Tish collapsed at Kat's side.

"I can't do this, Kat," she said finally, tears running down her face. "I can't. Those nice people. All those lies."

"What lies, Tish?"

"All those things I said. All that, that..." Tish stopped, her hand to her mouth.

"Truth?" said Kat into Tish's sudden silence.

The pain in Tish's eyes almost broke Kat's heart.

"Wait here."

Kat went to the car, got Tish's purse, and brought it back.

"Blow your nose."

Tish rummaged in her bag, found tissues, and did as she was told.

Slowly she calmed down.

"They've always been like this, you know," she said finally. "Maggie. Matthew. Or Madison and Carlisle. What stupid names. Who wants to be named after cities rather than people?"

Tish wiped her nose again.

"What does it say about me that I have such ungrateful, selfish, insufferable children?"

"You can always say they take after Fitz," suggested Kat.

The strangled sound Tish made might have been an attempt to laugh.

"And you say they've always been this way?" asked Kat. "Maggie and Matthew?"

"Always," said Tish sadly. "Ever since they were old enough to say 'mine,' it's been almost their entire vocabulary." She made a disgusted face and shook her head.

"All they ever want is money. That's all they ever think about. Just like Fitz. Daddy I need. Mommy I need. Yet they both have so much! It's Luke who needs help. My sweet Luke. And he never asks for anything."

"He's a lot younger, isn't he?"

Tish nodded. "Nine years."

"How'd he turn out different?" asked Kat.

"He..." Tish stopped. "I guess I just got it right the third time," she finished softly.

She sighed deeply.

"Are all families like this?" she asked, after blowing her nose again. "Aren't families supposed to be the people who give you love and comfort and support?"

"I don't know," said Kat. "I lost mine a long time ago."

Tish looked at her, shocked. "I'm sorry. I didn't know."

"No reason you should."

"Your mother's church…"

Kat shrugged and looked across the acres of grass. The endless acres of loss and pain.

"Tell me something, Tish," she asked after a moment. "Why did you decide to sell the diamonds out of your rings rather than the other stones?"

Tish was quiet a long time.

"It was Maggie," she said.

"Maggie?"

Tish produced a small nod. "Always wanting money. Always nagging Fitz for jewelry. Do you know she badgered me for my rings when she married Teddy? Teddy." She shuddered. "She said they should be my wedding gift to her. We paid for that wedding! Cost a fortune. Then she trashed the dress. That horribly expensive dress. She said all the girls were doing it."

Tish rolled her shoulders and looked across the expanse of green. In the distance, behind a hillock, they could hear the whine of a riding mower.

"She just made me so angry. Going on about how Fitz should have left me years ago. Her sheer *greed*.

"When she said my jewelry was *hers*, suddenly I wanted to get back at her." She glanced at Kat. "Horrible, isn't it? What kind of mother wants to get even with her child like that?" She shook her head sadly.

"And—if I'm honest?—I really didn't want them anymore. I never really wanted rings like this. All show." She looked down at the rings on her finger. "You can probably guess they were Fitz's idea." With the fingers of her other hand, she rocked the rings back and forth. It was a gesture that Kat had seen before, usually when Tish was dealing with Fitz. "I wanted an Art Deco-inspired design, set with a ruby," she said wistfully. "I still have the drawings I made."

Tish huffed and looked up at Kat. "Suddenly, I just knew our original story wouldn't work. Why would I want to raise money to leave my husband with that miscellaneous bunch of diamonds when I had this," she waved her left hand, "on my hand? Well, obviously I wouldn't. I couldn't lie and say they were CZs. Any jeweler looking at them would know they weren't."

Tish shrugged. "So now they are. When we do this again, I can honestly say these are CZs. And we can sell more big stones at one time."

"You are brilliant, Tish," said Kat after a minute. "You are absolutely brilliant. And absolutely right. Any jeweler who might buy those stones would wonder that. I never thought about that."

"I feel so bad about the Markers."

Kat shook her head. "I don't think you should. I think Mrs. Marker wanted to give you full price."

Tish was surprised. "Why do you think that? She doesn't know me."

Kat shrugged. "Just a feeling. That maybe she, or someone she loved, had been in an abusive relationship. Maybe someone had helped them. Or maybe someone hadn't."

"I'm not in an abusive relationship," said Tish. "I just made that up."

Kat kept her eyes on Tish's. Tish stared back for a long time.

"I am, though, aren't I?" she finally whispered. "I have been for a long time. First Fitz. Then Maggie and Matthew. No," she said, as she turned to watch a car drive by. "First my parents." In the cluster of trees behind them, a woodpecker drummed on a tree.

"You must think I've been very stupid," she said, unable to meet Kat's eyes.

Kat turned away, too, and tried to control her face. *No, she thought. Stupid would have been me.*

"You said you lost your family a long time ago," Tish continued. "I'm beginning to wonder if I ever had one. Except for Luke."

"Tish. You are a big-hearted woman who has tried to make the best of a difficult situation, and who loved her children unreservedly. As a mother should." Kat paused to steady her voice. "That doesn't make you bad or stupid. It makes them all both bad *and* stupid."

She laid her hand on Tish's. "I have the smartest, bravest person I could possibly have in this mess with me."

Tish looked at Kat, then smiled.

"I have to ask," said Kat, a quizzical look on her face. "Why did you say you couldn't act?"

Tish frowned. "I never said that."

"Yes, you did. When you told me about doing costumes. You said you hadn't been on stage. You said you couldn't do that."

"Oh," said Tish. "That." She turned away and fussed with putting tissues back into her purse.

Kat waited, curious to see if Tish would answer her question or change the subject.

Tish snapped her bag shut, then gazed across the cemetery lawn. Her right hand plucked nervously at the grass between them.

"Honestly?" she finally said, still not looking at Kat. "I always thought I'd be a good actress. But..." There was a long pause. The lawn mower had stopped or just moved so far away they couldn't hear it.

Tish took a deep breath. "When I signed up to audition, the teacher said… He said…" Tish's face flushed pink. "He said I wasn't right for the stage. I told him I hadn't even auditioned, so how could he know?"

Now she looked at Kat, her dark brown eyes smoldering almost black. "He said 'zaftig' women couldn't act. He meant fat. He said if I could sing, I could try opera, where they were more tolerant of 'zaftig' women. He assigned me to the stage crew."

"What. A. Turd," said Kat. She shook her head. "All I can say is he should have been there today." She looked straight at Tish. "Because you would have shown him you are one *hell* of an actress."

Tish's smile was sunshine. "I am, aren't I?" she said.

She started to laugh, and they both laughed until they cried.

CHAPTER 25

CONFESSION AND SUSPICION

"Oh, look!" said Kat, pointing, as they came out of farmland and crossed a small river into Wilmington.

"What?" said Tish, startled. "What am I looking at?"

The women had sat side by side in the cemetery for a long time, talking some, but mostly sitting quietly, until Tish's face wasn't blotchy anymore and she felt she could face the world. After purging the long-held poisons from her heart in her confession to Kat, her mind had cleared, leaving her feeling...buoyant. She hadn't had anyone she could talk to for years. And Kat had really listened.

But, as they'd headed south, something Maggie had said had popped up in her mind. Now it kept running through her head, so she hadn't paid much attention to the country they were passing through.

"I think it's called the Gemini Giant," said Kat. "I didn't know it would be right at the side of the road. We have to stop."

Kat pulled into the parking lot and stopped.

Tish started to laugh. "This?"

"Absolutely." Kat got out of the car.

She walked over to the 30-foot fiberglass sculpture of a man wearing a bilious green jumpsuit and a silver helmet that would have looked futuristic in the 1950s. The rocket he held was emblazoned with the name of the restaurant on the other side of the parking lot: The Launching Pad.

"Why?" asked Tish, following Kat.

"They're a classic part of Route 66," she told Tish. "They were all over. Somebody used them originally to advertise mufflers," she pointed up, "not rockets. So, they were nick-named Muffler Men."

"And people—like you—stop to see them?" Tish was incredulous.

"People come from all over the *world* to see them," said Kat.

"Again, I ask, why?"

"Route 66 is part of American history, Tish. Westward movement. Dust Bowl. After the war, everyone had money. They had cars. They wanted to explore. Car companies exploited that. And roadside attractions, like this one," she pointed a thumb at the giant by her side, "were part of it. They got people—especially people with children..."

"Again, like you," said Tish.

Kat laughed. "*Exactly* like me... to stop, buy a burger, buy a souvenir, pay a dime to see a, I don't know, a dinosaur footprint. Then they'd talk about it back home and more people would come out and buy more burgers and souvenirs and spend more dimes. And dollars." Kat patted the figure on the leg. "Gem the Giant here was part of the scheme."

"You know all this because?"

Kat's smile dimmed. "My dad. He and some friends drove the Route when they were eighteen. Before it was decommissioned. He always promised to take me." She took a deep breath.

"I'm sorry," said Tish.

Kat shrugged. "Long time ago." She patted the giant again.

"So," said Tish, trying to lighten the mood. "Am I right in thinking you're going to get me to stop at all of these?"

"You have no choice," grinned Kat. "I'm driving. And yes, as many as I can find."

"Food first. Too bad this place is closed right now."

"Then we'd better find something that's open."

Ten minutes later, Tish was enjoying a burger at the Polka Dot Drive-In in Braidwood. They'd already toured the fiberglass figures of 1950s pop icons, like Betty Boop and James Dean. They were sitting at a picnic table under the awning where carhops used to deliver food to parked cars.

"I always wanted to have lunch with Elvis," said Tish, looking across the asphalt at the fiberglass replica of The King. She looked back just as Kat reached over and snitched a french fry from the paper basket in front of Tish. "You should have bought your own. I would even have treated."

Kat wrinkled her nose. "Not really hungry," she said, dipping the fry into ketchup.

Tish ate a french fry of her own, swallowed, and looked at Kat. "You didn't eat that much at breakfast. You have to be hungry."

"I'm not really a big eater."

Tish frowned as Kat nibbled at the fry. Did she hear criticism about her own meal in Kat's remark?

"So where should we go from here?" asked Kat.

"You're the tour guide," said Tish. "But I'm not up to trying another sale. I'd just like to stop somewhere. Regroup."

Kat nodded. "I agree. Check your phone. See what's available for the night at the next biggish town."

Tish's gaze caught Kat's eyes. "Are you paying for tonight's room, too?" she asked lightly, but there was tension in her voice.

"Me?" Kat sat up in surprise.

"Yes. Remember? Your 'walking around' money."

Kat frowned. "You just made a big sale. I thought we agreed that our expenses would come out of the 'inventory' sales."

"Those were *my* diamonds," said Tish thornily. "They weren't inventory. That money is mine."

"Apologies," said Kat contritely. "You are absolutely right." She snagged another french fry.

"Unlike your 'walking around money.'"

The hand holding the french fry stopped inches away from Kat's mouth.

"The money in the safe, remember?" asked Tish, her tone absolutely serious now. "The street-buy money? The money Maggie wanted so desperately?"

Kat swallowed. "That was part of the generous bonus you gave me for not suing for wrongful termination, wasn't it?"

Tish heard the attempt Kat was making to keep her tone light and teasing. But Tish was through with being manipulated.

"*Gave* you?" she hissed.

It was mid-afternoon and the restaurant was slow. There was no one sitting near them under the awning. However, they were still in a public place. It wouldn't pay to raise her voice.

"You took it and never told me! You never put that on

the table when we counted everything out. There must have been $20,000 in that pouch."

"$16,275," said Kat. "And that was the *least* of what I was owed. It doesn't even begin to cover what I could have earned..."

Kat stopped and stuffed the french fry in her mouth.

"Could have earned? What do you mean?"

"If I'd gone somewhere else."

"What do you mean, if you'd gone somewhere else? You never said you were looking for another job."

Kat shrugged. "It didn't pan out," she said, but she didn't meet Tish's eyes.

Tish's eyes narrowed speculatively, and her well-honed prevarication meter—what Luke called her "fib finder"—went into the red zone. There was an evasion here, but she couldn't quite figure out what it was.

"I thought I was supposed to be the banker. You trusted *me*, you said," she finally said to Kat.

Kat opened her mouth, but Tish interrupted. "But maybe I can't trust *you*. Since you've already skimmed $20,000...

"...$16,275..."

"...off the top."

"Look," said Kat, wiping salt and grease off her fingers. "Cards on the table. When you opened the safe that night, I had no idea how it would go. I didn't know if I *could* trust you. I thought I could, but... Well, neither of us had exactly been in that position before. At least I hadn't been. I assumed the same was true for you." She gave Tish a fleeting smile, but Tish wasn't about to be mollified. Kat went on. "So yes. I kept the street-buy money."

"And didn't think to tell me, even now when we're

crim..." She stopped. Looked around her. Lowered her voice. "Criminals?"

"We are not...what you said. I did not cheat you. Because Tish, I *was* owed that money. I was owed my final paycheck—one month's pay, *plus* my unused sick and vacation pay, *and* the bonus Fitz promised."

"That's not..."

"And," said Kat, cutting her off, "most companies cover medical insurance for a few months—especially," she said, as Tish tried to interrupt again, "in the case of a wrongful termination." She wiped her fingers again. "A lot of that money really is mine. Owed to me before you opened the safe."

"But not twenty...$16,275," said Tish tightly.

"Okay. Maybe not all. So maybe I didn't put that money in the bag. Maybe I didn't discuss it with you. But Tish, I *did* use it to pay for the motel, our food, our disguises, and gas. I *have* used it for 'operating expenses.' And you never objected. Even when you knew it was mine."

Reluctantly, Tish had to admit, Kat was right. She'd never asked about the money used to pay for everything for the last few days. She'd been too busy dealing with the—literally—overnight change in her life to think much about it. Kat had said she had the cash and she'd paid. And Tish had let her.

But she wasn't ready to let it go yet. "You think I'm supposed to be grateful?" she said.

"Maybe not grateful, but a damn sight less hostile, now that you know," said Kat. "Because a *lot* of that money was mine legitimately."

"When were you going to tell me?"

"I..." Kat sighed and her shoulders dropped. "I don't know. I wanted to last night. I just couldn't quite figure out how. I couldn't slip it into the bag. I knew you'd spot it immediately."

Kat reached across and filched another fry.

"When you reimbursed me the hotel money, back in Chicago... I just didn't know what to say." She paused and swirled the fry in ketchup. "I guess Maggie did me a favor, sort of, reminding you about it," she added, and bit the end off the fry.

That could be true, thought Tish, taking a deep breath, then sighing it out. But she was going to have to keep an eye on Kat.

"If that was an apology, it still doesn't give you the right to snitch my fries," she said.

"Sorry," said Kat. "I really am sorry, Tish. I should have owned up at the beginning."

Tish nodded slowly. "Fine. So far. But that money goes into the suitcase tonight, minus what you were *legitimately* owed by Superior, including bonus, medical insurance for six months, and whatever we would have paid into your 401K. The rest is to be used for 'operating expenses' while we travel and sell the stones. At the end, it will be part of the split, which you agree is 35% for you and the rest to me."

"Plus the Kashmir sapphire," said Kat.

"And the sapphire. When we get to California, we divide all the cash accordingly and go our separate ways."

"We do."

It can't come soon enough, thought Tish.

So why did the thought make her so sad?

CHAPTER 26
THE CALL

Kat docked the Buick at the curb in Pontiac, Illinois, near the B&B they'd rented on the town square. They looked out the windshield at the wall-sized mural in front of them.

"You planned this, didn't you," asked Tish, after a moment.

"I swear I had no idea," said Kat, grinning. "But I can't say I don't like it."

The mural featured a bright yellow, 1950s era automobile that appeared to drive into the wall and onto Route 66 toward the silhouette of what looked a bit like Disneyland in the distance.

The big yellow 1957 Buick now parked in front of it looked like a publicity stunt.

Tish's phone buzzed like a rattler. She picked it up as gingerly as if it were one.

Kat leaned over to see the ID.

"If you don't answer it, he'll keep calling. Or worse, they'll come looking for you," said Kat.

"I know, but...I'm afraid I'll sound guilty."

The phone buzzed again.

"No, you won't. Believe me. Something happens to you when you get on stage."

"But..."

"You can do it."

Another buzz.

Tish took a deep breath, swiped the connection open, and hit speaker.

"Hello?"

"Mrs. O'Donnell?"

"Not for long," said Tish, letting anger seep into her voice. "Is this Detective Chung? You've been leaving me messages."

"Yes, ma'am. This is a wellness check. Are you okay?"

"Of course, I'm okay. Why wouldn't I be?"

"Well, your husband said you didn't show up for work today."

"Of course, I didn't show up for work today." Now she added irritation. "Why should I, when my soon-to-be-ex-husband of thirty-five years tells me he's leaving me for someone half his age? Why on earth would he, or anyone else, expect me to go to work like everything was normal?"

"When you weren't at home, and no one had heard from you..."

"I had no reason to stay, did I? And no desire to ever talk to Fitz O'Donnell again in my life."

"Your husband said you had a fight. The house was in a bit of...disarray," said Chung. "I want to be sure you are safe and unharmed."

"I was upset. I threw things. Unfortunately, I don't have an accurate arm. Or it would have been Fitz who was harmed."

There was a pause.

"Where are you, ma'am?"

Tish's heart rate ratcheted up. "I'm staying with a friend."

"Would you mind telling me where?"

Tish's grip on the phone tightened. "I do mind. I have no intention of you telling anyone where I am. All you need to know is that I'm okay."

"Were you aware, Mrs. O'Donnell, that there was a break in at the jewelry store you and your husband own?"

"Yes. My daughter called to tell me."

"What can you tell me about that?"

Tish sighed in exasperation.

"Just that she was more concerned about getting money to pay a credit card bill. She spent most of the time screaming about me walking out on her father. I hung up on her."

"Ma'am, I meant what can you tell me about the break in?"

"About the break in? Nothing." Tish's hands were starting to sweat, but her voice stayed calm and steady. "It was news to me when Maggie called."

"You don't sound upset, Ma'am."

"It's not my store, Detective. It's my husband's. It's his problem."

"Ma'am, there was no sign of forced entry, and neither the vault nor the safe were forced. In fact, it seems like it was someone with knowledge of the store."

Tish's head snapped around, and she stared into Kat's startled blue eyes. "Vault?" mouthed Kat.

"Ma'am?" asked Chung when their silence had drawn out. "Ma'am, who at the store would do that?"

Tish turned back to the phone and, to her surprise, one name came out of her mouth, tinged with acid.

"Fitz."

"Your husband, Ma'am? Why would he rob his own store?"

"Because I told him I'd take him for everything he has in a divorce." Tish let all her anger out. "You tell him it won't work. My attorney will find it. She'll find where Fitz has hidden everything. When we're done with Fitz O'Donnell, he's going to be working a drive-through in a paper hat. You tell that to that lying, whining, thieving snake. Now, if you or Fitz have any more questions, call my attorney."

She thumbed the phone off with a shaking hand and dropped it in her lap. She sat there breathing hard. Her heart was beating so erratically, she felt dizzy.

The phone buzzed again.

Tish let it go to voice mail.

Kat gave her time.

"You are terrifyingly brilliant," she said, once Tish was breathing normally again.

"What do you mean?"

"You just gave Fitz to the police."

"But we know it was us."

"*We* know it was *us* for the *safe*. But you're right. It had to be Fitz for the vault."

"Why would he do that?"

"Easy. Insurance. To pay Clapham and whoever else he's double dealing. Or to make up for the cash we took from the safe. He and Hilary need money to run away on."

"Then why call the poli... Of course. He needs their report for the insurance," said Tish, answering her own question. She rubbed her forehead with the fingers of both hands. "He'll be in for a shock. The safe isn't insured. I've told him that for years."

"And he can't tell anyone what was really in it," said Kat.

"I need to walk," said Tish, tossing her phone in her purse and reaching for the door.

"We need to unload fir…" Kat started to say, but Tish slammed the door on the end of her sentence and started striding down the sidewalk.

Kat caught up with her as she rounded the corner. "Are you all right?" she asked.

"I don't know," said Tish, oblivious to the exquisite, classic brick courthouse in the center of the square. "How should I know? I'm not even sure who 'I' am right now. So how should I know how 'I' feel?"

She didn't expect an answer, and Kat, wisely, didn't try to give her one.

After a couple blocks, they'd walked out of the neighborhood of old, brick-fronted buildings surrounding the courthouse square and were passing duller buildings housing city services.

"Any idea where we're going?" Kat finally asked.

Tish looked around. "No, not really."

"I don't mean to push, but I don't like to leave the car with everything in it for long," said Kat.

"Frankly, right now, Kat, I almost wish someone would steal the whole thing," said Tish bitterly. She sighed. "I wish we could just go back to last week."

At the next cross street, Kat touched Tish's arm. They both stopped.

"That would be easier," she said. "But barring that, I think our only choice is forward."

"Is it?" asked Tish. She looked at the Presbyterian church across the intersection, with its golden bricks and arched windows. "Maybe we could just give it all away."

Another statement that had no answer.

"Maybe we should head back, unload, and get something to eat," said Kat.

"Will that change things?" asked Tish.

Kat shrugged. "We won't be hungry."

Tish looked at her. "You're never hungry anyway."

"Always a first time," said Kat.

"If you say so." Rather than turning around, Tish turned the corner. She still had anger to walk off. And fear.

At the end of the block, she stopped abruptly.

"What..." Kat started to say, but the words dried up.

The building directly across from them was a Catholic school. Standing next to it was a steepled, red-brick Catholic church.

Tish closed her eyes and felt safe and centered. She knew what she had to do.

CHAPTER 27
ANOTHER CONFESSION

Tish sighed, her shoulders dropped, and she moved forward.

Kat panicked.

"Tish... No..."

She ran to catch up.

"Tish, where are you going?"

"I'm going to see if they have evening Mass," she said.

Kat caught her arm.

"You can't be going to confession."

Kat had had nightmares about Tish spilling their burden to a priest.

Tish turned angry eyes on Kat.

"You know, Kat. I'm getting tired of you telling me what to do. Where we'll go. What you're going to take, and what I'm going to get. Who I'm going to talk to. You are no better than Fitz."

Kat felt her jaw drop.

"You will *not* tell me when and where I can go to church, or what I can and cannot share with my priest."

Tish yanked her arm out of Kat's hand, spun around, and marched down the block to the front of the church.

Kat went after her with no idea of what she would say. She slowed and stopped when Tish went up some steps and into a side door.

Now what? Kat wondered, feeling lightheaded. *If Tish tells the priest about the store...*

Do priests have to report confessed crimes to the police? She didn't think so, but they could certainly pressure a guilt-laden woman to report the crime herself.

What should she do? Everything was in the car. She could just take it and go. But how long would that last if Tish decided to turn herself in?

Feeling sick, Kat stepped off the sidewalk into the shade of a row of trees, intending to leave the few french fries she'd had at lunch in the garden at the church's foundation.

Instead, she found herself face to face with the Virgin Mary.

There she stood in her soft blue robe, calm and compassionate, hands spread welcomingly.

Kat had given up on the Catholic Church when her mother had died. But her mother had always trusted the Virgin, and surprisingly so did Kat.

Her panic settled. She stood in front of the statue, hands clasped at her waist, leaf-filtered sunlight warm on her shoulders, and closed her eyes.

Blessed Mother Mary, she said in the sanctuary of her mind, *Please help me...*

As she unburdened herself to the Virgin, she was dimly aware of cars passing at the intersection. Footsteps clattered up and down the sidewalk behind her and the stairs nearby. The church door opened and closed several times.

She gradually became aware that someone was standing next to her wearing Shalimar. She opened her eyes and turned. She and Tish looked at each other for several heart beats.

"Confessing?" asked Tish.

"To someone who will never tell," said Kat. "You?"

"Same."

Kat was dying to ask what the priest had said, but as Tish was calm, and she didn't hear any sirens coming their way, she decided to leave it alone. For now.

"Hungry?"

"I am," said Tish. "Wasn't there a place with a patio near where we parked?"

"Hmm," said Kat, as they turned back toward the center of town. "We should be able to see the car from there."

They'd gone about a block in silence, when Kat said, "You weren't in there very long. No Mass?"

Tish looked at her strangely. "No. No Mass. But I was almost an hour. I expected you to storm the gates."

"Almost an hour?"

Tish nodded, and her eyes softened. "You could have come in with me."

"So, no Mass, no priest?" Kat persisted.

Tish bristled. "What you really want to know is, did I confess," she said, stopping in the middle of the sidewalk.

"I didn't say that."

"No, but that's what you want to know."

Kat did, but she said nothing, simply held Tish's gaze.

Tish sighed. "No. No priest."

Relief relaxed muscles Kat hadn't known were tight.

Then Tish smiled a bit wickedly. "I talked to a very nice nun, Sister Anne."

Kat's relief vanished, and her stress level shot to the

clouds. A conversation with a nun wasn't protected by the seal of the confessional.

It was over. The rest of her life would be in prison.

"I told her what you'd said at Saint Mary's of Chesterkovia."

"Czestochowa," corrected Kat automatically.

"Well, that explains why she laughed when I said it," said Tish.

"What I said? What did I say?" Kat clawed frantically through memories of the church, her prayers, the times with her mother.

"About the Holy Mother knowing all about life on the run," said Tish.

Kat clamped her molars. She didn't dare ask what had precipitated that conversation.

"She agreed with you."

"She did?" Kat stared. "A nun?"

"I've found most nuns are pretty down to earth," said Tish. "Mostly I talked about my kids."

"Your kids?"

"Hmm. She told me to pray for them and to keep loving them. Even if I didn't like them much." Tish smiled sadly.

Kat stared at her while her mind calmed. Maybe she wasn't going to prison.

"Then she left me to do some of that praying." Tish looked away at a passing car. "While I was doing that, I realized you were right," she said, without looking at Kat. "I can't go back. I can only go forward."

Tish hadn't confessed. They weren't going to prison. Kat's prayers had been answered.

Thank you, Mother Mary, she said fervently in her heart.

"Let's go forward then," said Kat.

They crossed the street and cut across the lawn alongside the courthouse. They stopped at a bronze Lincoln casually leaning on a rail fence, his heel hooked over the bottom rail, coat over his arm, top hat perched on the post. Totally at ease, iconically Lincoln.

"Is there no escape from Lincoln?" asked Kat, smiling.

Tish lifted her shoulders, hands held palms out and up. "It's Illinois," she said, and they both laughed. It felt good, thought Kat, after the emotional roller-coaster of a day they'd had.

But when they reached the corner of the courthouse square nearest their car, they stopped laughing.

There was a crowd of people around the Buick.

Two people stood by the rear bumper taking a selfie with the car mural in the background. Several others waited their turn. Across the street, a man and woman walking a dog were pointing and smiling.

"I should have parked somewhere else," said Kat. "That mural..."

"You said no one would notice the car on Route 66," hissed Tish.

"Oh, Uly, look," said a woman's hushed voice behind them.

"Ain't she a pip, Erm?"

"We got to get a picture. We've never seen one that cherry."

"Looks like we're not the only ones."

The couple squeezed past. "'Scuse us," he said.

The man glanced over and nudged Tish. "If you want a photo, I'll be happy to take one for you," he said, winking. "I'll bet you're real photogenic."

"I hardly need one," said Tish, pulling away from his presumptuous elbow. "It's my car."

"Say! No kidding?" said his wife, who stopped and turned back. "Don't suppose you'd consider selling it?"

"Not on your life," said Kat, before Tish could respond. She caught movement out of the corner of her eye. Her head snapped around. "Hey!" she shouted at a couple of young men who were stepping up onto the car bumper. "Hey! You! Get off the car!" She started down the block at a trot.

"Thought you said it was your car," the man called Uly asked Tish. "She sure acts like it's hers." But Tish was already running after Kat.

The two men were about to sit on the trunk lid, when Kat confronted them.

"I said, get off the car," she told them.

"Keep your shirt on. We just want to get this shot," said one, raising his arm phone in hand.

"You heard her. Get. Off. The. Car," repeated Tish, coming to Kat's side.

"What are you getting so worked up about?" he said. "We're not hurting anything."

"Screw this," muttered Kat, heading for the driver's door.

"I'd suggest you get off now, while you can," said Tish to the two bumper trespassers.

"Or what, lady?"

Suddenly the big engine roared. The car jerked forward. The wise guy's arms flailed out, knocking into his friend. Thrown off balance, they both leaped to the ground.

"Hey! What do you think you're doing?" one of them yelled at Kat.

"Starting the car," said Tish, as Kat threw the big car into reverse and started rolling it back. "We did warn you." Tish smiled at them, and ran to get into the passenger seat, slamming the door.

Kat slid out of the space, scattering photographers.

"We have to find some place more inconspicuous to park," said Kat.

"This car is never going to be inconspicuous," said Tish. "We should have taken the Mercedes."

CHAPTER 28

THE CRUSH

Kat and Tish settled into a patio table at the restaurant. They'd unloaded their luggage and found another parking spot a block away that they could see from where they sat. It wasn't far from the first parking spot, but it didn't sit in front of a provocative mural.

All we need is for someone to steal the Buick, she thought.

They might as well take her heart.

"Why didn't your dad install an alarm system in that car while he was doing all the restoration on it?" asked Kat, after they sat.

"I have no idea," said Tish. She waved her hand dismissively, eyes fixed on the menu.

"Why do you dislike the Buick so much?"

Tish looked up. "Why should I like it? It was my father's car, not mine." She set the menu down and leaned forward. "All my life, I heard the story, about how he bought that car to celebrate after his father died and left him the store. His father died, Kat. He celebrated. With a car."

"Wow. No love lost, I guess."

"None. He and my grandfather were always at each other's throats, from what my mother said. Granddad Ryan had to have everything done his way, from the way the store was run, to who Dad married, to what he drove. Dad buying that car was his first act of rebellion. Though it's hardly rebellion if the man you're rebelling against is dead. Especially if you turn out to be just like him."

Tish sat back and shook her head.

"I get the feeling you and your dad weren't close," said Kat.

"Nope. The business should have been mine. I thought it would be mine. But when I got married, he gave everything to Fitz, because Fitz was a man and more capable of taking care of everything." Tish glared down the street at the Buick. "Except for that dam...stupid car. Oh, no. When he died, *that* he left to me."

"Why? Cars are usually guy territory."

Tish snorted. "Fitz once made a snide remark about the kind of men who drive old cars. My dad said he'd decided to keep the car 'in the family.'"

"He didn't want to keep the store 'in the family'?"

"*That* was business. Men's stuff," said Tish scornfully. "Getting the store didn't mean Fitz was family. At least not family enough for the car."

"So why didn't you sell it?" asked Kat.

Tish was silent for a solid minute, looking across the square to the big yellow and white convertible.

"I don't know," she finally said. "Maybe because it was the only thing my father ever gave me." The wistfulness in her voice sent a knife through Kat's heart.

Tish sighed. "Or maybe the practical side of me realized that if I ever wanted to sell it, it was cash in the bank."

"That and your jewelry would give you a fresh start almost anywhere," Kat said softly, not saying aloud the question in her head: *So why burgle the store?*

There were only two answers to that: One, revenge. Two, blackmail, to get Fitz to drop Hilary.

"Yes," said Tish, her eyes coming back to Kat. The look in her eyes confirmed Kat's suspicions that the raid on the safe hadn't been about the money. Or at least, not *all* about the money.

"I've never heard you talk about your family much," said Kat.

"We weren't a very warm family," said Tish sadly. "Except for Grandma Geraghty."

"Ladies, have you decided?" Their waiter hovered by the table, turning their water glasses upright and filling them.

Tish shook herself and ordered fettucine alfredo with chicken. "And a glass of your house wine," she said.

"I'll have a salad," said Kat.

"Which one, ma'am?" asked the waiter.

"Just the small green..." Then she saw Tish's face.

The betrayed look of a woman, always worried about her weight, trying to enjoy rich Italian pasta in the company of a size three woman eating a salad.

"... salad, to start," she amended. Frantically she tried to recall the menu, which she'd already handed to the waiter. She took a stab at an Italian standby she was sure would be there. "And lasagna," she added. "No wine for me this evening." She glanced at Tish and smiled. "I'm driving."

Tish smiled back, and Kat felt ridiculously pleased not to have embarrassed her.

"Very well," said their waiter. "I'll be back with some bread and your wine."

Kat shook out her napkin and put it on her lap.

"I'm glad you're finally eating something," said Tish. "You shouldn't starve…"

"Well, howdy," said a jovial male voice. A sunburned hand covered with reddish blond hair dragged out the chair next to Tish. The man called Uly, whose wife had asked about buying the Buick, dropped into it. His wife settled into the one next to Kat.

The couple were in their early sixties, Kat guessed. Uly was not much taller than Tish, gray stubble on a chin gone soft. His pants were hitched low, allowing the developing belly, which poked through a gap in his shirt, room to breathe.

"Excuse me?" said Kat, shocked that strangers would just invite themselves to sit down.

"Uly Armentrout," he said, sticking his hand out to Tish. She automatically reached for it. Kat could see she regretted it immediately. "Hope you don't mind. This little red-haired beauty caught my heart before, when we met on the street. Couldn't resist sitting down to get to know you—you both—a little bit better."

"We're having a private conv…"

"Don't mind Uly," said his wife to Tish, talking right over Kat. "I don't. He's just the biggest flirt. But he really means no harm. I'm Erma, by the way." She put a hand out toward Kat. Kat resisted the urge to shake hands. Erma didn't seem to notice.

Erma had probably been a cheerleader in high school, but the intervening years had ruined the figure of a girl who, Kat stole a look at Tish, had probably always been a little heavier than fashion dictated was acceptable. She had a sweet face under Tammy Faye makeup, and blonde hair that had been over-dyed to the texture of attic insulation.

"We eat here every time we drive down Route 66," said Uly. "Better spaghetti than even Erm makes. What's that sauce you get, babe?"

"Oh, that would be telling, Uly." She turned to Kat confidentially. "The secret is mixing 'em up together. Get lots of different spices that way. And I always add black olives."

"We buy the big take-out size here and eat at the hotel while we watch some TV. It's nice and relaxin'. Make sure you get some of that bread, too. You two stayin' here local? Maybe we can eat together. Our room's pretty big. We always get a king-size bed." He winked at Tish and patted her hand. "Know what I mean? So, what's your name, honey?"

Tish snatched her hand away and looked helplessly at Kat, who was equally at a loss. The Armentrouts' thick hides were impervious to barbed hints they weren't wanted.

"She's Mary. I'm Kate," said Kat. No time to come up with better names or stories. Those would have to do.

"Katie. Mary. Glad to know you," said Uly.

Kat winced. She hated being called Katie.

"While we got you both here," said Erma. "I wanted to talk about that cherry Buick you have over there." She nodded at the car parked a block away.

Kat made a mental note to move the car again. Maybe across the state.

"I was serious before," Erma went on, "when I asked if you wanted to sell it."

"To you?" Kat's astonishment was tinged with contempt, and she knew it.

The insulting tone slipped right off the Armentrouts.

"It's not for sale," said Tish, "to anyone."

"We'd give you a good price," said Erma.

"No," said Tish.

"Mr. Armentrout?" The waiter had arrived holding a large white bag in his hand. "Family-sized spaghetti and two mostaccioli?"

"You didn't forget that bread now, did you?" asked Uly, standing.

"No, sir." The waiter handed him the bag.

"Why don't you get your dinner to go?" suggested Erma, reluctantly getting up. "Join us and we can talk about driving the Route."

"Say, maybe we can make up a caravan, drive it together!" said Uly.

"What makes you think we're driving Route 66?" asked Kat, dismayed.

Uly lifted his chin in the direction of the Buick.

"Can't have a car like that and not drive the Mother Road," he said. "Would almost be a crime." He grinned and Erma chuckled.

Kat froze. *Crime?*

They were saved by their waiter returning with their bread and Tish's wine.

"We're having our dinner here," said Kat. "Privately. It's a lovely evening. And we have things to discuss."

"Private things," reiterated Tish.

"Well, I'm sure we'll catch you somewheres else," said Uly. He leaned down and leered a wink at Tish. "I look forward to seein' this little cutie again."

"Yep. See you on the road," said Erma.

"I hope the hell not," muttered Kat, as the two unwanted guests swayed toward the exit.

Tish picked up her glass. "You should rethink the wine," she said, and took a swallow. "I'm thinking about a second."

"You could be right," said Kat.

CHAPTER 29

THE PAWN SHOP

"You chickened out!" Tish practically crowed, as they got into the Buick. "Admit it! After pushing me into it at the Markers', you chickened out!"

They'd just pulled away from a pawn shop near downtown Springfield.

"I did not chicken out."

"You did! After putting on this act like you knew what you were doing. Bwaaak bwak bwak bwak," clucked Tish.

"I did *not* chicken out. Not like you mean. I told you. It was the wrong place."

"It was perfect. Did you see how nicely everything was displayed? They had plenty of diamond jewelry."

"A place that well kept is probably squeaky clean. Also proof it wasn't right."

Tish snorted. "It was right enough that you dropped eight hundred bucks on a laptop and printer."

"They also had plenty of cameras, inside and out," said Kat. "And did you notice how carefully they were checking IDs?" The big, well-lit store had been busier than Kat had expected for a Wednesday afternoon, too. Too many witnesses.

Kat shook her head. "It was definitely the wrong place."

"So? We knew they'd check IDs. We have a story. It worked with the Markers."

"This wasn't the Markers'. No one there had a sympathetic ear. With all the guns they had, I bet they get checked constantly by the police. Springfield is the Illinois state capital, after all. And the Capitol building isn't all that far away. They're hardly going to be lax with the threat of terrorism everywhere. Which means a pawn shop—at least *that* pawn shop—is very careful about their records."

"Like we were, at Superior, when we bought jewelry off the street," said Tish thoughtfully.

Kat nodded. "Exactly. The Patriot Act. That pawn shop is probably also looking for money-laundering schemes." She sighed. "At the very least, they'd probably have refused to buy from us. At the worst, we'd have been busted."

"But they're pawn brokers."

"Tish, pawn brokers aren't idiots. They're just like jewelers. There are good ones and...not so good ones. Jewelers like to look down on pawn shops, but a lot of jewelers started that way. Didn't they?" She stopped for a light and turned to look directly at Tish.

"Fine. Touché," said Tish. Kat could see that her partner was irritated she'd remembered that Tish's grandfather had started his business as Superior Jewelry and Loan.

"After the price of gold went crazy, a lot of jewelers went back to their roots. Before that, how many jewelers would buy jewelry off the street? Or, heaven forbid, put a sign in the window to advertise it?"

"I said all right! I still wonder how you know all this."

"Know what?"

"About pawn shops. About which ones are good and which are bad. How to look for cameras."

Kat shrugged.

"Instinct. Experience. Picking up on little tells." She smiled. "Mostly I learned it from caper movies. My dad and I loved watching them. We used to rent them or go see every one that came out. Even when they had subtitles."

Tish dropped her head in her hands. "We're going to die," she muttered indistinctly.

Kat grinned. "Oh, Drama Queen. We're not going to die."

"Fine," said Tish, head still buried in her hands. "We're going to jail. Just like the Blues Brothers."

Kat shook her head. "We are not going to prison, either." She pushed the thought of the old Joliet prison out of her head. Tish didn't see her cross her fingers on the steering wheel. "But we are going to have to be careful and alert."

Tish raised her head. "I'm not sure I can do this."

"Oh, pfft." Kat made a derisive noise. "You did it all the time at Superior."

Tish frowned. "What are you talking about?"

Kat slid her a sideways smile. "Oh, Tish. You told me your superpower was not getting lost. Your greatest superpower is people reading. You almost always knew when one of the staff needed time off or was ill."

Almost always, she added to herself.

"You always knew when a customer was sketchy or someone was lying, except..." She almost said *when it was your kids*. "...except when Fitz overruled you. Remember that engagement ring he bought? The one with the sapphire and six diamonds? 'Found in a parking lot'?"

Tish rolled her eyes. "He was so angry when I called the police about it. We didn't get the money back."

Kat paused. "Maybe neither of us should have been so surprised by what we found in the safe."

"You're right," said Tish pensively. "You're absolutely right. That sapphire ring was three years ago. I wonder how long this has been going on."

Good question, thought Kat. Fitz probably wouldn't have tried scamming one criminal, let alone two, without some previous practice. What else had flown below Tish's—and Kat's—radar?

"Why don't you find us a place to stay?" she said, changing the subject.

"The Wyndham is right downtown," said Tish, scrolling through her phone.

Kat shook her head. "Find a B&B where we can stay for three or four days," she said. "Remember to contact the owner directly to see if we can pay cash."

"I have two words for you: Room service," said Tish. "That place in Pontiac was cute, but it was above a coffee shop. Six a.m. they were grinding coffee!"

"I have one word for *you*: privacy. We have some paperwork to do, and it will take some time. I don't want people running in and out of the room. See if you can find a house in a quiet neighborhood, maybe one with a garage we can use." She flashed Tish a devilish grin. "Money is no object."

"Very funny," said Tish grumpily, searching her phone. "What paperwork?"

"Let's make a couple more stops and get settled in some place. Then I'll show you." *But you won't like it*, Kat thought.

"Why don't I find us a place to eat, first? I'm starved."

Kat smiled. "As long as we can park in front."

CHAPTER 30
KAT'S SUPERPOWER

Tish only frowned when Kat came out of the big box office supply store. But when she placed an online order at the library, Tish's eyes fairly jumped out of her head, as she glared her indignation at Kat from the neighboring desk.

Kat ignored her and kept typing.

Once back in the car, Tish exploded.

"That was more than $2000!" she shouted.

"Expenses, Tish."

"And another thousand for the shredder, the laptop, and the printer at the pawnshop, where we were supposed to be selling not buying."

When Kat reached for the ignition, Tish leaned across and gripped her hand. Hard. "What. Is. Going. On," she said through gritted teeth.

Kat leaned back and shifted to face Tish. Took a deep breath.

"We need stronger stories and documents to go with our disguises," said Kat.

Tish looked blank for a moment, then her eyes narrowed as the wheels turned.

"The laptop and printer and that gizmo you bought online?"

Kat nodded again.

"You're talking about faking IDs."

"Yep."

"Kat, that's...that's..." She stopped.

Kat raised an eyebrow. "Illegal?"

She shook her head at Tish's abashed look.

"You're going to have to lose the middle-class, Midwestern morals if we're going to succeed."

"Well, excuse me," said Tish, nettled. "I was taught that forgery was a crime."

"So's theft. And I'm not forging. I'm faking."

"Forging. Faking. And we agreed it wasn't really theft. I had a perfect right to take...something...out of the safe," said Tish.

"I agree, though I doubt Fitz would. Regardless, you wouldn't have been there if you didn't already have cracks in your middle-class, Midwestern morals. Otherwise, you'd have cried and tried to convince Fitz to come back or gotten an attorney and tried to fight fair. And you would have lost. You know that."

Tish tried to outstare her.

Kat stayed quiet and stared back.

"All *right*, yes! I would have lost" Tish's sigh blew the spiky bangs off Kat's forehead. "But sometimes, Kat, sometimes there just comes a breaking point. Don't you think?"

"I do," said Kat. "But until the other night, I didn't know you did."

"Well, yes. But how will we explain this if someone calls us on the fake ID?

We can't, thought Kat.

"Ah," she said, holding up a forefinger. "What you don't know is that *I* have a superpower."

Tish snorted. "You're going to tell me you're an expert forger."

"I am," said Kat, enjoying the look of shock on Tish's face.

"Well, not forger. Faker," she amended. "Forging is copying something real, like someone else's driver's license. Or money. Faking is faking. Making something not real that looks real. Like the passports you see in movies."

"You're splitting hairs."

"No doubt. But I made good money in high school making fake driver's licenses for kids who wanted to buy liquor. No one was ever caught." She shrugged. "I'll admit that the liquor stores near where we lived didn't look that hard. I made them bullet proof anyway. Some kids used them at bars in Bismarck, and they passed."

"Bismarck? You lived in North Dakota?"

"Yes. I was raised in Fargo."

"Your mom's church..."

"We left Cicero when I was six," Kat told her tersely. She should never have mentioned Bismarck. It raised too many questions.

"So how much money did you charge?" Tish finally asked. She seemed to sense Kat's reluctance to talk about her past.

"Fifty dollars each."

Tish whistled. "That *was* good money."

"And I made a lot of them."

"Things have changed," said Tish.

Kat nodded.

She didn't think it would reassure Tish to tell her that

she'd kept up with those changes through survivalists' websites and handbooks.

Tish sighed and put both hands up to massage her neck. "This just gets deeper and deeper, doesn't it?" She dropped her hands and turned to Kat. "Theft. Hot diamonds. Forgery. Fraud. Where do we draw the line Kat? Murder?"

"You're thinking *Thelma and Louise* again, aren't you?" said Kat. She shook her head and sighed. "Like I said. Drama Queen." She smiled at Tish to take the sting out of her words. "You wonder where Maggie gets it?"

Tish bristled, and Kat laughed.

"We aren't going to kill anyone, Tish. If you think about it, ours are pretty much victimless crimes. You took your divorce settlement, and I took my final check and bonus. Granted, more than Fitz planned on paying me, but you would have been more generous if I'd asked, yes?" She grinned.

"Not that generous," grumbled Tish.

"The diamonds you sold to the Markers were yours to sell. So, really, are most of the stones in the suitcase. When we sell them, we're selling what we have a right to sell."

The gold, though, will be a problem, she thought.

"What *I* have a right to sell," said Tish. "And you're rationalizing. No court would agree with us."

"You're right. On all counts. That's why we have to be sure not to raise suspicions." *And not get caught*, Kat added to herself.

"What about Clapham's diamonds? And the cash?"

"The cash is unidentifiable." At least Kat hoped so. "It's all used bills." She held her hands out palms up as if to say, *See? No problem.*

She dropped her hands. "I admit the one gray area is

when we sell Clapham's diamonds. But even those, Tish. We won't be misrepresenting them. We'll be asking a fair price..."

"They aren't ours legally to sell."

"Granted," said Kat. "Gray."

"Hardly gray," said Tish. "Right over into the red zone. We'll be selling stolen diamonds. Even if we didn't steal them."

"Deniability. They were in your husband's safe. You had the right to believe they were legit."

"Rationalizing again."

"Okay. We *suspect* they're stolen. So *dark* gray," said Kat. "But if we are careful and find pawn shops that are...less scrupulous than the last one, we should be okay. They'll sell them on and never check."

"With bullet-proof IDs."

"And caution," added Kat.

"Caution," echoed Tish.

As Kat pulled out of the library parking lot, she had a small quiver of apprehension. She didn't tell Tish that she'd left a small, possibly incautious trace of a trail in the library's computer.

CHAPTER 31

FITZ'S NO GOOD, HORRIBLE DAY

Fitz disconnected, set the phone down on his desk, and dropped his head in his hands.

The store was as silent as a tomb.

Appropriate, he thought. *I wish I was dead.*

The insurance agent had just told him, rather rudely, he thought, that they would not be honoring his loss claim. The police report had suggested that the burglary was the result of a family/divorce dispute, not a police matter, but something the couple would have to work out in court. In fact, the police wouldn't say for sure that there actually had been a burglary. Due to faint suggestions that one of the owners had emptied the vault, Jed said, there was even a slight whiff of suspicion of the intent to defraud the insurance company.

So, no. The insurance company was not only refusing to honor Fitz's claim, they were canceling his policies completely. Nothing in the store, including the building, was now covered. His cars were not covered. They'd also canceled his homeowner's policy.

So much for arson, he thought darkly.

Fitz sighed, picked up his phone, and dialed.

"Yeah, Pop." Carlisle answered on the second ring.

"They refused my claim," said Fitz.

"Well, not really surprising."

"You said it would work!"

"I said it was a long shot."

"They think I took the jewelry to defraud the insurance company."

There was a long silence. "You did," said Carlisle.

"You know what I mean."

"You should have gone with my first idea. Suggest that Mom took it all."

"Your mother?" Fitz guffawed. "Don't be ridiculous. No one would have believed she could have pulled off something like this." *For a smart guy*, thought Fitz, *Carlisle's not too smart about women.*

"You know that. I know that. But the cops thought she might be involved. The insurance company might have bought it, too," said Carlisle.

"Come on. Five minutes with your mother and anyone would figure that out."

"If you say so, Pop."

"But that's not why I'm calling. I need to get that jewelry back."

Another long silence.

"How can you expect to do that? You've told the police *and* the insurance company it was stolen."

"Yes, I know. But I need it. I had three supply companies on the phone this morning. I have no idea how they knew about the robbery. They acted sympathetic, but I could tell they wanted to know when they were getting paid. Then my employees started calling, wanting to know when they could come back to work. When I told them never, they all wanted final checks, severance pay, unused sick day pay."

Fitz nervously twisted his moustache. "Not only that, when I told our stone setter they'd all have to wait a while for payment, he got ugly. Threatened to get all the staff together, hire an attorney and sue."

Fitz had no intention of using the money for any of that. It was just a way to get Carlisle on his side. What he really needed was to get out of the country before certain people found out their property was gone. And he needed to salvage his relationship with Hilary by giving her a bunch of jewelry and getting her to Cancun.

Once there, he'd tell her they weren't coming back.

"So. Pay them," said Carlisle.

"With what? I don't know what they expect. It's not my fault I got robbed. On top of all that, your damned mother isn't picking up her phone," he added viciously.

"What are you calling *her* for?" asked Carlisle.

"People like *her*," he said snidely. "They wouldn't sue *her*. She's always bitching that the store should be hers. Well, let her have it if she wants it so badly. Let her deal with these people." *I'd tell her that, if she'd just pick up the damn phone*, thought Fitz.

"I still don't see what the issue is, Pop," said Carlisle. "It wasn't the bank that was robbed, it was the store. Surely you have enough in your business account to cover your payroll, expenses, and whatever you might need in severance."

Fat lot you know, thought Fitz. He'd been using the business account to pay for Hilary's condo. The memos on the check stubs had all been for business consultants, though Tish had been nagging him more and more about why the business wasn't improving if he was spending so much on consultants.

"Well, I don't," he told his son belligerently.

"Jeesus," said Carlisle on a long exhale. "It's your barista, isn't it?"

"None of your damn business. I just don't have the cash."

"Then start liquidating things."

"Like what?" Fitz snapped. "I need cash now. The house and the store building would take months to sell."

"What about that old gas guzzler of Gramps'?" asked Carlisle. "People pay a lot for old junkers like that. That's probably good for thirty or forty thousand. Maybe more."

"Tish took it."

"Mom? She hates that car."

Fitz had been shocked, too, to find an empty spot in the garage where the Buick had been. At least if she'd taken the Mercedes, he could have pressed charges for stealing his car.

Maybe she knew she could get more for the sixty-year-old Buick than he'd get for that five-year-old Mercedes.

"Yeah, well, hate it or not, it's gone. The only thing left is the Mercedes."

"The Corvette?"

"No can do."

"Why not?"

"I just can't."

He heard Carlisle sigh.

"You gave it to Hilary, didn't you?"

"She needed a car!"

"Still, it's in your name, isn't it?"

"Well. Yes. Technically." But Hilary would leave him if he sold the Corvette. It would have been one thing to sell it on their way to Cancun. She might have understood then. As it was, she was furious. She'd been questioned by the police. She didn't get any of the jewelry or the money or the trip to Cancun Fitz had promised. And now, Fitz couldn't even pay for the divorce she thought he'd promised. He'd had to give her something.

Fitz was frantic. He'd gotten into this mess for Hilary. He couldn't lose her now or he'd have nothing.

"No, Carlisle. I need the jewelry back. It's the only way. I can sell that for enough to get out of the co...the...the trouble I'm in with everyone."

"You realize, don't you," said Carlisle, "that as soon as word gets out you're selling the jewelry you claim was stolen, the insurance company will have you arrested and charged with fraud."

"Why?" squeaked Fitz. "They should be happy it was recovered. I'll withdraw my claim."

"Pop. You don't *have* a claim." Carlisle's spoke slowly, as if to a child. "They suspect you of attempting fraud. Suddenly getting the jewelry back and selling it will only convince them."

Suddenly, Fitz had a brilliant idea.

"You could lend me the money."

"What?" Now it was Carlisle's turn to squeak.

"Yes. You lend me the money. I pay off my staff and my suppliers. And later, when we can sell the jewelry, I'll pay you back." *Carlisle must make beaucoup bucks selling whatever it is he sells,"* thought Fitz. *He must have at least a few hundred thou in stocks or something.*

There was silence and heavy breathing on the phone.

"I don't think you understand my finances, Pop," Carlisle finally said slowly. "I never keep that much cash lying around. Everything I have is invested."

"So, sell some of it."

"Not that easy," said Carlisle stubbornly. "You also forget I'm going through a divorce. Marcia's lawyer is digging around looking at everything. If I start cashing stuff in..."

Fitz had had enough. "Look, *son*, you're in this, too, you know. In fact, this was your idea. I think you owe me."

For a moment, Fitz thought Carlisle had hung up, the silence hovered there between them for so long. Finally, his son replied.

"Let me look into it," he said in a measured tone. "But it will take some time."

"Don't take too long," said Fitz. *Because I may not have much time*, he added to himself.

CHAPTER 32

BUICK GROUPIES

"I don't know why we always need to sit by the window," said Tish. "Makes me feel like I'm in a fishbowl."

They were waiting to cross the street after lunch. They hadn't been able to park in front of the restaurant, and Kat had insisted on sitting where she could see the Buick, parked down a block at the curb on the cross street. Tish was still peeved.

"I just like being able to see the car," said Kat.

"You weren't this bad in Chicago," said Tish, as they waited for the light to change. A convoy of three heavy black SUVs rolled by, all the windows smoked and opaque looking. "I swear you're getting jumpier the farther we get from Evanston, as a matter of fact."

Suddenly, Tish realized she was talking to air.

"Kat?"

She turned. Kat was standing in the shadows of a recessed shop doorway.

"Kat?" she said again, as Kat slipped inside the store.

Puzzled, Tish followed.

191

Inside, by the front window, but out of sight of the street, Kat was watching the convoy turn at the corner.

"Kat, what is it? You're shaking."

Kat lifted her chin. "Those cars."

Tish looked out.

"What cars?"

"All those black cars."

Tish looked again, then turned back to Kat.

"What about them?"

"Don't they look suspicious to you?"

Tish turned to look again. The taillights of the last car were disappearing into traffic.

Frowning, she looked back at Kat and shrugged. "No. It's probably the governor."

"Governor?" Kat looked at her blankly.

"Springfield? State capital? Governor?"

"Oh," said Kat. "Yes. Governor." She inhaled shakily, and Tish realized she hadn't been breathing.

"What did you think it was?" asked Tish.

Kat shrugged and opened her mouth but was interrupted.

"Well, hey, pretty lady! This is my lucky day."

Tish turned to look into the scruffy, beaming face of Uly Armentrout.

"Erma," he called into the store. "Look who I found. It's our favorite lady road trippers."

Kat murmured, "Shit."

"I knew you had to be around the minute I saw that Buick," said Erma, walking up to them, her hands full of mugs, T-shirts, and caps. "We started looking right aways. We figured you'd come in here. Most everyone does."

That's when Tish and Kat looked around them.

"Souvenirs," said Tish.

"Route 66 souvenirs," added Kat. She closed her eyes. "Swell."

"I think they're going to make us honorary customers soon," said Uly, grinning.

"Well, enjoy," said Tish, yanking on Kat's arm. "We're late for an appointment."

"Oh, say, you're on vacation! No need to have appointments and hurry off," said Erma, smiling, but Tish saw something else in the woman's look she couldn't place.

"Can't be late! Got a buyer for the car," said Tish, as she pulled the door open.

"But you said..." The closing door cut off whatever Uly was going to say.

The two women powerwalked to the curb, looked both ways, then scurried across the street between batches of traffic. Kat had the keys in her hand.

"Do you see their car?" she asked Tish.

"I wasn't looking for it."

"Look for it now," she told Tish.

"How can I look for it? I don't even know what it is."

"It's one of those hideous blue Nissan Cubes. The juice box on wheels."

"How do you know that?"

"I saw them drive it away in Pontiac." Kat unlocked the passenger door and ran around to the driver's side.

Tish turned in a circle scanning the block. "I don't see it," she said.

"Then let's hope they're parked far enough away we can lose them," said Kat. "Get in."

As Tish buckled up, Kat turned the key. She slipped the big car smoothly into traffic, turning at the first signal, and again at the next.

"Where are you going?"

"Anywhere. Just trying to lose them."

"You said we'd be anonymous on Route 66 in this monster," said Tish. "Less conspicuous than in a big city, I believe were your words. Now it seems like every time we turn around, they're behind us."

"I didn't count on anyone like them," said Kat. "Vintage car groupies."

"Well, what do you know?" said Tish in mock tones of astonishment. "Something you aren't right about."

Kat didn't respond. She turned the car again, left this time, just skating through the light. Tish checked the side-view mirror.

"I don't see them," she told Kat.

Kat double-checked in the rearview, then took a deep breath. Her shoulders dropped, and Tish realized how tense she'd been.

After a couple more random turns, however, Kat glanced over at Tish. "Maybe it's not the car. Maybe it's you."

"Me?" gasped Tish.

"Could be," said Kat, her face serious. "He seems totally smitten. I think he's drawn to you."

"He's married!"

Kat tipped her head questioningly.

"So...? Maybe they're both attracted."

"*What?*" Beyond the one word, Tish was speechless.

"Or maybe they're interested in both of us. He did mention that big bed."

"Kat Merevec, you can't be serious."

Kat grinned. "Maybe not." Then she laughed.

"You are reprehensible."

"So true," said Kat, and laughed harder.

"Where's the B&B, oh navigator with the built-in

compass?" Kat asked, when she'd finally caught her breath. "You said they have a garage?"

Tish glanced out the window, caught the name on the nearest street sign. "Left at the next corner, down two blocks, and then right about a half mile," she said grudgingly.

"Right. Let's get Beauty under cover as soon as we can." She glanced at Tish again, her eyes dancing behind the big lenses. "And you, too, since Uly seems able to sniff you out."

"Oh, just...just drop dead," said Tish distinctly.

Kat roared with laughter again.

CHAPTER 33

THE INTERLUDE

"It's beautiful out there," said Tish, sliding open the patio door and stepping into the rental house. The backyard was private, quiet, with carefully maintained shrubs and trees and a patio set that Tish planned to put to good use. "This might actually be like the vacation you promised. Except we still have to cook."

"You made a good choice, then," said Kat distractedly. "And there's always takeout." She was already in the formal dining room that she'd made into her office. The plastic ID printer had been delivered by express mail the day after they moved into the house.

"Can I borrow your phone a minute?" she asked Tish.

"Who are you calling?"

"I'm going to the library to use their WiFi. I don't want to run the risk that the Armentrouts will spot the car again. I'm going to call a cab."

"The house has free WiFi," said Tish. "Why not use that?"

"Traceability," said Kat.

Tish stopped asking questions and handed Kat the

phone. She didn't want to know any more. She couldn't exactly claim ignorance if they were caught with phony IDs while trying to sell the diamonds and other gemstones, but she was going to ignore what was going on in the dining room for as long as possible.

After Kat left for the library, Tish made iced tea and went out to sit on the patio. The day was perfect. Not a cloud in the sky. The breeze was pleasant and the humidity was low. She might stay here the rest of day.

She put her bare feet up on the lounge, leaned back, and closed her eyes. She was half asleep in the quiet when her phone buzzed. She checked the caller ID warily. After Maggie's tirade and the interrogation by the police, Tish was leery of incoming calls.

It was her younger son, Luke. They'd remained close, even though he now lived in Oregon with his husband, Jess.

She slid open the connection.

"Luke," she said happily.

"Congratulations, Mom!" was the first thing he said.

"What? Why?"

"You finally left him. Hooray for you! I'm so glad."

"You're glad?"

"Of course, I'm glad, Mom. Dad has treated you like a servant for as long as I can remember. When Maddie-Mags told me, I cheered. I think it upset her," he added. She knew he was grinning.

Maddie-Mags, thought Tish. *I wonder if he calls her that. She'd hate it.*

"Maggie told you about Hilary...?"

"Yep. Glad to hear it. She'll pick him clean and throw him out. He'll be lucky if she doesn't pluck out his gold fillings. I'd make a special trip back to Illinois just to see that."

"Oh, Luke..." Tish choked, relieved. She'd lost Matthew

and Margaret years ago somehow, and she'd become as reconciled to that loss as any mother could. But it would have broken her heart beyond repair to lose Luke, youngest of her three children, and by far her favorite. She blinked hard.

"So, what are you going to do now?" he asked. "Do you have a good attorney? Jess can probably recommend one."

For the briefest of moments, Tish thought he was talking about a criminal attorney, not a divorce specialist, since Luke's husband practiced criminal law. She came within a breath of telling him the truth. Just for that moment, she wanted someone—other than Kat—to tell her that what she'd done was okay, rational, reasonable—and justifiable in a court of law. To tell her there was a way out of this mess.

In the same instant, though, she had the strangest feeling... That she was standing on the edge of a deep canyon. She could step back into the desert her life had been...or she could step forward and fly.

She wanted to fly, to swoop into the canyon and see where it went. To reach out with her wings and touch the sky. To see what was on the other side.

I must be out of my mind, she thought.

"I'm still working that out," was what she finally told her son.

"Are you okay?" asked Luke. "You sound...I don't know...different."

"Yes, Luke. I'm truly okay." Tish realized she was smiling.

"Well, you know that anything you do is okay with me. Can you tell me where you are?"

Again, she hesitated. But it would be wrong to involve him in this.

"No, honey. I don't think I will. Not right now. If anyone asks, you can honestly say you don't know."

There was a hesitation on the other end of the phone. She knew him well enough that she could almost hear him change mental gears.

"Mom? Are you in trouble?"

"Sweetheart, I guess that remains to be seen."

Another pause from Luke.

"There's something you're not telling me, isn't there?" said Luke finally.

If you only knew, thought Tish. "There's probably quite a bit I'm not telling you, at least right now," she told him. He'd said anything she did was okay with him, but this? And him married to a criminal lawyer? Tish couldn't risk it.

"Are you at least with a friend?" Luke finally asked.

Now that's a tricky question, thought Tish. "Yes, I am," she finally said.

"Good," he told her. "Anyone I know?" She heard him smiling.

She laughed.

"No, I'm not with a man friend, if that's what you want to know. And I know that's what you're asking."

"Darn! I was hoping you had a younger model, too." Luke laughed. "As long as you're safe and with someone you trust, that's all that matters to me. Are you okay for money?"

Here was the difference in her children, she thought. Maggie and Matthew had buckets of money, yet neither of them had offered her help. Luke, struggling from gallery show to teaching gig, would have sent her all he had.

"I'm fine, sweetheart. Don't you worry about me."

"Okay. Stay in touch. Call me if you need anything. And let me know if you need that lawyer. Love you, Mom."

"Love you, too, Luke."

Tish sat in the beautiful backyard that was not her own, in a house and town that were not her own, in a life that was not her own—at least not yet. And still. She felt that all the world was hers.

She listened to the birds for a long time, while her life and her sense of self re-shaped itself around her, and she basked in her son's love.

CHAPTER 34

TISH MAKES A CHANGE

The next day dawned overcast and still. By the time Tish got up, the temperature was rising and so was the humidity. She was already damp with perspiration when she came downstairs lugging a bulging trash bag and her winter coat. She dropped the bag in the hall and laid the coat over the top.

"Feels like a storm is coming," she said to Kat, who was already in the dining room at the laptop. "I think we might need the AC today."

"Hmm," was the response.

Tish fiddled with the thermostat and heard the unit kick on. Then curiosity got the better of her, and she looked over Kat's shoulder at the computer screen. A larger than life-size image of a Missouri driver's license was there surrounded by all kinds of complex icons and codes. "Kitty Carter," was written in the name space, and a birthdate that must be Kat's, an expiration date of next year, and all the other minutiae found on legal documents everywhere.

"No photo."

"No." Kat sat up, stretched, rolled her shoulders. "We'll

have to get some taken today or tomorrow," she said. She looked up. "You changed your hair."

Tish's red hair, usually piled up on her head, was down, held back in a clip but reaching almost to her shoulder blades.

"I got tired of messing with it. Though it's so muggy, I might change my mind. Put it up and get it off my neck."

Kat looked at her for a long moment, and Tish thought a smile grew around her eyes.

"I'm going out," she said, and Kat's look changed to surprise.

Then she noticed the bag in the hall. "What's in the bag?"

"I decided I needed a change," said Tish. "There's a recycle shop that agreed to look at some things. If they don't take them, I'll donate them somewhere."

Kat looked at the bag again, then looked up at Tish.

"The coat?" she said, raising an eyebrow.

"The coat," said Tish.

"I thought you couldn't live without it."

Tish shook her head. "It wasn't that I couldn't live without it, it was that it was so expensive when Fitz bought it that it felt wrong to leave it."

"That all?" asked Kat.

Irked, Tish said, "No, that's not all. I thought I'd do some window shopping. Get lunch. Maybe tour the Capitol building. With your permission, of course."

"Want me to drive you?" asked Kat.

"I think I can just about handle getting there on my own." Tish pointedly did not ask Kat to come. She wanted time to herself, time to just...be. There had always been demands on her time, whether it was work, or jewelry industry socializing, or things to do for the children. When she shopped, she power-shopped: shirts for Fitz, shoes for a business trip. She never just...shopped. Looking in windows, checking out specialty stores, having coffee on her own.

At least she hadn't for... Oh, she couldn't remember how long.

"You taking the Buick?" Kat asked carefully.

"It *is* my car," said Tish testily, snapping back to the present.

"Maybe." Now Kat did smile. "But it's *my* soul mate."

Tish sighed. "You and my father. No. I don't want that monster. I called a cab. Just like you did."

At that moment, the yellow car stopped at the curb in front.

"Back later," she said and turned.

Tish was almost at the door when Kat called after her. "If I'm gone when you come back, I may go for a run. Do you have a house key?"

Tish rummaged in her purse, found it, and pulled it out.

Kat nodded. "Later then," she said and bent forward to the computer again.

Tish hesitated a moment, glanced quickly at the storage cupboard under the stairs where they'd stashed their "inventory," then back at Kat. She reached a decision, picked up the trash bag and coat, and went out the door.

FREED OF THE CAR, Kat, and her responsibilities, Tish had a wonderful time. The clouds lifted, a breeze came up and the day became pleasant enough that she enjoyed walking around downtown.

The cab dropped her at the resale store. But instead of selling her clothes, she ended up trading them for the kinds of things she'd never bought for herself before, either because her parents wouldn't have approved, or they weren't appropriate for work. Bright colors. Cropped pants. Sandals with flowers on them. Vacation clothes.

Bags in hand and her heart light, she decided against the Capitol tour, found a café with outside seating near the Old State Capitol, and watched tourists come and go. She'd always wanted to go to the Lincoln Presidential Library and Museum but was now stymied by her shopping bags.

Then, smiling to herself, she realized she'd learned something from Kat. She walked over the Wyndham, explained the situation to the desk clerk, tipped him a twenty to store the bags until he went off his shift. The two hours she spent going through the mesmerizing, high-tech museum had been worth it. She was still dazzled by it when took a cab back to the B&B.

"Kat, I'm back," she called when she unlocked the door. Then she heard the shower. *Kat must have gone for her run,* she thought.

It had been such a free afternoon, on her own, obligated to no one, that for a mutinous moment, Tish hesitated by the cubbyhole under the stairs. She peeked inside. The suitcase was there. Kat was in the shower.

I could just go, she thought. *Take the Buick and go. Nothing is holding me here. Everything in there is really mine anyway.* She eyed the suitcase.

She couldn't do it. Something had changed, somehow. She and Kat were now a team. Each had skills the other needed. Kat had a world view that would—with luck—get them through this. And she, well, she'd keep them disguised and make sure Kat didn't get lost.

There was a tug on her heart, too, something that felt like...friendship. Kat had been kind, after Maggie's call. Kat annoyingly teased her about Uly Armentrout, like a friend or sister would do.

Yes, she'd also tried to skim almost $20,000 off the top of their cash, but, when Tish had confronted her, she'd seemed truly...remorseful.

Maybe Kat was feeling tendrils of friendship, too.

Tish closed the cubby door and took her new clothes up to her room. She could get used to B&Bs if it meant she could have her own room. She passed the bathroom where the door was ajar about eight inches to let steam out.

The shower shut off while Tish was changing into a new skirt and a blouse with capped sleeves. *How retro*, Maggie would have said, she thought, rolling her eyes.

Well, so am I, thought Tish, smiling.

She went down the hall to show her new outfit to Kat.

Through the open bathroom door, Tish could see Kat standing in her bra and panties in front of the mirror. Her underclothes were rosy purple, sexy, silky and edged with lace, because, of course, Kat would have sexy, colorful—and matching—underwear.

Tish could see her cupping her breasts—still erect and firm—gently stroking them, staring at them in the mirror.

Suddenly Tish felt dowdy in her gently used, "retro," resale clothes and practical cotton underwear. Stepping away from the bathroom, she went back into her bedroom, closed the door, and leaned on it, willing the tears not to come.

"Money is no object," Kat had said, but Tish, ever frugal with her "middle-class, Midwestern morals," had felt clever, trading in her unloved clothes for something brighter, more casual, something closer, she'd thought, to who she wanted to be.

Now all she felt was cheap.

The rosy glow of the day was gone. She wished she'd taken the suitcase from the cupboard downstairs and run while she could. What would Kat think of her? Kat, ever stylish in her sexy underwear, her trendy, spiky, purplish hair. Her perfect tits. How could she have thought that someone like Kat could want to be her friend?

"Someone you can trust," Luke had said. That's what friends were.

Could she trust Kat? Tish didn't know. She didn't really know Kat. She said caper movies had taught her all these things about surveillance and not leaving traces behind. She'd also said she had "instinct and experience." What kind of experience gave someone the ability to make fake IDs and find shady pawn shops?

Who was this person she was suddenly dependent on? This person she had to trust?

"Tish?" Kat knocked on the door behind her head. "Are you in there?"

Tish wiped the tears away and cleared her throat.

"Yes," she said. "Just changing. I'll be down in a minute."

"I thought we could grill that chicken, if that sounds good to you. I can start the grill."

"Sounds fine." Tish tried to make her voice sound cheery.

She heard Kat move away.

Tish had always been quick to trust people, to think they were her friends. That had always been her weakness. But when had she last really had friends? High school?

Once she'd married, Fitz, the kids, the store had been her life. There hadn't been time for friends. They had industry associates, and dinners with sales representatives and other jewelers. Who among them were her friends?

Who did she call or email, have coffee with? Fitz objected to any time she wasn't focused on him. She'd thought that was what marriage was supposed to be.

What did that leave her with now?

Myself. The thought rose slowly in Tish's mind. *Only myself.*

But who, she wondered, was she?

THE GOLD

After a sleepless night, Tish stumbled down to breakfast the next morning. She'd come close—multiple times—to calling Fitz, telling him everything, begging him to take her back, begging to start again.

Just a few days ago, she might have. But something had shifted, and though she'd picked up her phone several times, she couldn't make the call. She wouldn't humiliate herself like that. For better or worse—and where had she heard *that* before?—she was in this thing with Kat.

She found Kat in the dining room, a brilliant red, embroidered shawl around her shoulders; they'd left the AC on the previous night, and the house was cool this morning. The inventory suitcase lay open on the table in front of her. She was holding a one-ounce gold ingot, rubbing her thumb over it, but she was staring at the middle of the table.

Panic and anger surged though Tish.

"What are you doing?" she snapped.

Kat seemed to pull out of a trance. She blinked rapidly and looked up at Tish.

"Doing?" she asked.

"With the gold."

Kat looked down, as if surprised she was holding it. She shook her head.

"Thinking about what you said about it. The gold."

"I don't remember what I said," said Tish irritably. "Is there coffee?"

Kat nodded as Tish walked stiffly into the kitchen. When she came back, steaming cup in hand, Kat was still holding the ingot.

"Beautiful shawl," said Tish more calmly, as she sat down next to Kat where she could surreptitiously see and count the ingots in the bag. "I haven't seen you wear that before. You're usually all in black."

"My mother's," said Kat, surprising Tish.

"So, what did I say that's bothering you?" asked Tish, when Kat said nothing more.

"Why the ingots?" said Kat. "You said yourself the store buys ready-to-use, milled gold products for the shop."

Tish shrugged and sipped her coffee, then made a face when it burned her tongue.

"Why do these have a Superior hallmark on them?" asked Kat. She slid the ingot across the table to Tish. "Do refiners do that for jewelers?"

Tish picked up the ingot and shook her head. "I really don't know. But they wouldn't have to. We have all the ingot molds and marking equipment in the shop."

"You do?" asked Kat, surprised.

"Sure. My grandfather bought gold during the Depression, remember? He refined it and made his own wire and sheet stock and casting grain. He made ingots, too."

"Why?"

Tish looked up at Kat. "Easily transportable. Easily exchangeable. Easily hidden. Smaller than wads of cash. Remember the times and the place, Kat. Just outside Chicago? Prohibition? Capone may have had his stronghold down in Cicero, but there were plenty of other bootleggers and speakeasy owners. Other people selling drugs and running gambling halls."

"Of course," said Kat. "Money laundering. Trade the cash for gold. Trade the gold for more of what they were selling."

"Or hide it," said Tish.

They both looked at the gold in Tish's hand. Fitz *had* been money laundering, thought Tish. There was no other explanation.

She felt a chill. If he'd been caught, by virtue of being his wife, she would have been implicated. She might still be at risk.

"Sooo," said Kat, gesturing at the ingot. "This is most likely what's left of the gold jewelry that Clapham's diamonds came from."

"Probably a good guess." Tish sighed, her temper cooling. She looked at Kat. "Kat, I truly did not know this was going on," she said. One of their jewelers must have known, though, Tish thought suddenly. Someone pulled those diamonds out of their settings. And it wasn't Fitz.

It was probably that damned Justin, she thought, *that Maggie had a crush on.*

"I know you didn't know about it," said Kat.

"You do?"

"You called the police about that sapphire ring, remember? I know you wouldn't have put up with this."

"No. I wouldn't have." What would she have done,

though? Tish wondered. Would she have been able to call the police on Fitz?

Tish rubbed her forehead. "How much is there again?" she asked.

"Twenty-two one-ounce ingots. That's almost two pounds, right?"

Tish nodded. "Two pounds in Troy weight. On the bathroom scale, it would be probably," Tish closed her eyes, and rocked her head back and forth slightly as she did the conversion in her head, "closer to a pound and a half," she said, opening her eyes.

"So... At current gold prices?"

"Roughly forty thousand dollars." Tish didn't even have to think about that. She checked the gold market every day at work.

"That we can't touch."

It was now Tish's turn to stare into the distance. She thought for several minutes, then shook her head. "I don't know how. If Fitz has been making these to sell..."

"...or give back to Clapham..."

"...or that," agreed Tish, "if we try to sell them, it will come back to us. Won't it?"

"I don't know how it wouldn't," said Kat. "If Fitz was supposed to give the ingots back to Clapham—which makes sense for all the reasons you mentioned before about hiding it and trading it—then even if we managed to sell them at a coin shop, Clapham would surely hear about it. Eventually." She hesitated. "In fact, once he finds out Fitz has been robbed, he might well put the word out to certain pawnshops to look for the ingots, for just that reason." She reached over and tapped the ingot lying in front of Tish. "With Superior's logo on them, they'll be readily recognizable."

"So, if we try to sell them, even if we aren't arrested, Clapham will know who has his gold. And, by extension, the diamonds," said Tish.

Kat nodded.

"What do we do?"

Kat sighed, picked up the ingot, and tossed it into the bag with the others. "I suggest we go out to breakfast." She snapped the suitcase shut and stood. "Then we need to get passport photos so I can finish our documents."

"About the gold," said Tish, irritated.

Kat shook her head. "I don't know, Tish."

She suddenly seemed to see Tish for the first time, her eyes taking in the lightweight lavender sweater and dark violet, lavender, and pink skirt. "Is this another new outfit?" she asked curiously.

"Yes," said Tish, suddenly wary.

"It's very nice. It suits you." Kat picked up her cup and headed to the kitchen, leaving Tish perplexed.

CHAPTER 36

MISSING

"Try her one last time," said Detective Sam Lyons, pulling up at the curb in front of a nondescript corner unit in the new condo development on the edge of Evanston.

"You're the boss," shrugged Detective Adam Chung, dialing. "But she hasn't answered for the last five days, I doubt she'll answer now." He put the phone to his ear and listened.

"Humor me. We don't have a warrant. I just want to talk to her. Be sure she's okay. It tends to backfire if you want someone's help but surprise them in their underwear."

"I thought you were convinced it was a domestic issue. That you were going to let them squabble it out in court," said Chung, as Kat Merevec's phone rang.

"I still think that." Lyons drummed her long, slim fingers on the steering wheel of their car. "But I don't like the fact that this woman disappeared at the same time O'Donnell 'fired' her, and now we can't reach her. Not only that, she didn't come in for her last check or return the store keys."

"So maybe she's involved?"

"Not impossible," said Lyons. "If she was fired, it could be a revenge robbery. She certainly wouldn't have needed that last check if that's the case. But she'd sure have to have planned it fast. And she'd have to get in and clean out both the vault and the safe between 8 a.m. when the time lock clicked off and maybe 8:45 when O'Donnell called in the robbery. It would be very high risk. I can't see one person pulling that off. It would have to be a team. And I can't really see that here."

"So. You think maybe she came in early, found O'Donnell or the wife taking everything, and they shut her up?"

"Also possible. Or they bought her off. If that's the case, though, then why didn't O'Donnell just stop with telling us he'd fired her? Why tell us she hadn't picked up her last check? Or that she still had the store keys?"

"He doesn't strike me as the sharpest knife in the drawer," said Chung.

Lyons lifted an eyebrow but didn't comment. "I just don't like that we have two women we can't account for."

"We've talked to O'Donnell's wife."

"You reached the O'Donnells' younger son?" asked Lyons. "You're sure the woman you spoke with was Mrs. O'Donnell?"

Chung nodded, cut the phone connection. "No answer. Yeah. He talked to his mom a couple nights ago. Says she's okay. Told him she's staying with a friend."

"Where?"

"He claims she wouldn't tell him," said Chung.

Lyons shook her head. "What a family." She pushed open the car door. "Okay. Let's go. You've got the key?"

They'd stopped at the rental agency on their way over to the condo.

Chung held it up and they went up to the front door. He knocked, then rang the bell. Waited.

"I hate this part," said Chung, inserting the key into the lock. "I always expect to find a body."

"Sometimes there is one," said Lyons. "You never get used to it."

Chung swung the door open. "Hello?" he called.

From the quality of the silence, Lyons knew no one was home, and the sterile smell told her there was no body.

"Okay. No one home. No one dead," she said. "Let's see if it looks like she's robbed a jewelry store and run. You take this floor, I'll look upstairs."

Chung nodded and moved into the living room.

Lyons was back downstairs in less than ten minutes. Chung was just closing a few cupboard doors in the kitchen.

"Looks like she was planning to come back," he said to Lyons. "Coffee maker is set up for the morning. Food in the fridge. Not just condiments, but makings for a fresh salad. Leftover takeout boxes. Juice container partially full. It's also weird that there's a small office off the living room, but it's empty. Not like anything's been taken, but like nothing has ever been there."

"No furniture? Blinds half open? So light comes in, but no one can see in easily?"

"Yeah," said Chung. "How'd you..."

"Same upstairs," said Lyons. "The spare room is empty. Only the bedroom has furniture in it. Clothes are there in the closet and the dresser. If something is missing, I can't see it. Suitcase is still on the shelf. All the toiletries you'd expect are in the bathroom, no empty spaces on the cabinet shelves. Nothing seems to be missing."

Lyons frowned and shook her head. "I like this less and less," she said. "Did you find a laptop?"

"Nope," said Chung. He waved a hand toward the small desk in the corner of the living room. "All the usual stuff. Her checkbook is there, but no computer, no laptop, tablet. Nothing but the big screen there and the internet connection."

"How about her purse?"

Chung shook his head. "No. I checked the closet." He pointed to the kitchen. "The door there goes to a garage. Her car is gone, so she probably has the purse and phone with her."

"So why isn't she answering that phone?" said Lyons, almost to herself. "And why hasn't she come back from wherever she went? Did O'Donnell really fire her? Is she blackmailing him and now he's trying to blame her? If robbed the store and disappeared, why not take her things?"

"Not much anyone would want to take," said Chung. "Looks like she placed a bulk order from IKEA."

Lyons looked at Chung. "What kind of car does she drive?"

"Gray Hyundai Elantra. It's leased. Just made the June payment.

"Rental agency says the condo rent is current as well," Chung added. "On a one-year lease, renewable each year. Agent said she's been here six years. They keep trying to get her to buy, but she's not interested."

Lyons squinted at Chung. "She's been here six years. Has a good job. Makes good money. But she has an apartment she doesn't own that's half empty. A minimum of clothes." She looked around. "And nothing personal. I saw no pictures upstairs and none down here."

"Could be on her phone," said Chung.

"Could be," said Lyons. "But most people have at least a few prints of family or friends or even themselves on vacation. And look around." She waved an arm. "No plants. No tchotchkes. It could be a B&B rental."

"Neat enough for one," said Chung. "There wasn't much in the cupboards, either."

"Hmm." Lyons turned slowly, her eyes raking the apartment. "This doesn't feel right," she murmured.

"Put out an alert for her," she finally told Chung. "Ask the state police to look for the car. And track down her phone. I'll feel better if we find her."

"If we can't?"

"Then I think we're going to have another conversation with Mr. O'Donnell."

CHAPTER 37

THE SHADY SHEIK

itz was sprawled at the dining table, staring at a bowl of soggy cereal and a half a cup of cold coffee, and missing Tish's omelet and bacon breakfasts, when the phone rang. Desperate for Carlisle to call, he snatched it up without looking at the caller ID.

"Mr. O'Donnell," said the too-familiar electronic voice. Fitz's stomach fell. "You haven't been taking my calls."

"Sorry about that," said Fitz, trying for a tone of jovial exhaustion, but hearing only nervousness in his voice. "We've had a bit of a disaster here. I've been dealing with that."

"I don't like the sound of 'disaster,' Mr. O'Donnell. Especially if your disaster becomes my disaster."

Fitz wracked his brain, but there was no way to sugar coat this. It had been in the papers. His unwelcome caller had to know, so lying would be a bad idea.

"I'm afraid my store was robbed over the holiday weekend. They got everything."

"Everything." The voice was flat. But it always sounded

218

flat passed through whatever electronic device he was using to disguise it.

Fitz tried to swallow but found his mouth spitless.

"I'm afra…" his voice croaked. He cleared his throat. "I'm afraid so. All the stones and jewelry. Uh, all the cash"

There was a long silence.

"What I believe you are saying, Mr. O'Donnell, underneath all the drama, is that you have neither my money nor my diamonds. Do I assess the situation correctly?"

Fitz would have preferred yelling. He could handle yelling better than this flat, calm, oh-so-reasonable restating of the facts.

"I'm afraid so," Fitz told the voice.

"I believe fear is the appropriate response here, Mr. O'Donnell."

The voice let that hang, as Fitz felt the urgent need to piss.

"Look, I can get your money back, I just need some time."

"The time has passed, Mr. O'Donnell. You were to deliver my diamonds last Monday. Yet you have ignored my calls and have made no attempt to contact me, though this 'loss' has been in the newspapers for several days."

Unfair, thought Fitz. *The guy's got his number blocked. How does he expect me to call him? Not that I would have…*

"Yes, well, as I said…" Fitz started to say.

"I have been patient, Mr. O'Donnell, but my patience is not without end."

"No, no, of course it isn't, and I apologize for this set back. I'm working on getting you your money." He tried to force a chuckle.

"My money?"

"Well, yes, I assume you want your money back, since I can't deliver the diamonds."

"Our agreement was for the diamonds, Mr. O'Donnell."

"Well, yes," Fitz said again. His shirt was soaked through, and the phone was slipping in his hand. "But getting diamonds to replace the ones that were stolen, well, sir," Fitz groveled, "well, that will take me much longer."

Like never, thought Fitz. *I don't have money to buy them legitimately and going back to Clapham is out of the question.*

Not to mention deadly.

Another silence. Longer this time. Fitz's gut roiled. He got up and went to hover over the kitchen sink. He was sure his coffee was going to come up.

"How much longer?" the voice finally asked him.

Fitz opened his mouth to blurt out the first thing that came to mind but stopped just in time.

Time. He needed time. Carlisle said it would take time to cash in his investments.

He wiped one hand on his pants, then switched the phone to wipe the other hand.

"I'm trying to arrange a private loan," he said. He tried to sound confident, but it came out pleading. "A...a friend is going to cash in some investments..."

"That may take more time than I have patience for, Mr. O'Donnell," the voice said sharply. It was the first emotion he'd heard from this shadowy figure.

"A month," blurted Fitz. "Just another few weeks."

Another long silence flowed through the phone to lay like a load of gravel on Fitz's navel.

"I'm unhappy, Mr. O'Donnell. Very unhappy."

I'm going to die, thought Fitz.

At least it wasn't Clapham. The unarticulated threats from the voice on the phone were frightening, but

Clapham... Clapham didn't have to make threats. Clapham just had to exist. Like a black hole.

"Three weeks, Mr. O'Donnell. You have three weeks from today. I will call you then to arrange delivery."

"Of course. Thank you. The money will be here."

"Not the money, Mr. O'Donnell. I told you. Our deal was for the diamonds."

"Yes, yes, of course. The diamonds. I won't fail. I do apolo..." Fitz stopped babbling when he realized he was talking to the air.

He set the phone, clattering, down onto the counter. He wiped both hands on his pants again. Three weeks. Surely Carlisle could unload some of his investments in three weeks. Even if he had to take a loss.

All Fitz needed was enough to get him and Hilary on a plane headed south. Carlisle could sell the jewelry to get his money back. He had rich clients. Then he could send the rest on to Fitz.

Fitz laid a hand on his belly. The coffee he'd been drinking for three days felt like it was going to burn a hole out the side of his stomach.

If it wasn't the voice that Carlisle had dubbed the shady sheik, it was Madison going on about her credit card and Tish's jewelry, or Hilary nagging at him about the engagement ring she didn't have, the divorce he didn't have, and the trip to Cancun that hadn't happened.

He leaned on the counter, hanging his head. *How did this get so fucked up? It was all going so smoothly. I'm supposed to be on a beach right now—Cancun, Bahamas, I don't fucking care as long as it isn't here.*

Goddamn, Tish. Who knew she'd fucking *leave*? This should have been her problem. And a safe in her fucking closet! She'd never mentioned a safe. They were married, for the love of Christ. She shouldn't be hiding something like a *safe* from him.

What the hell did she have in there? He'd been wondering that for days. Madison kept whining on about her jewelry, but Fitz only knew about the jewelry in the box on the dresser. What jewelry had she been hiding in the safe?

He had to get her back. He'd promise her the store. That's what he would do. He'd promise to sign over the store to her. Let Tish deal with lawsuits and voices on the phone and an empty vault. She wanted the goddamned store, she could have it. If he could get Tish back, this would all go away.

This pain in his gut would go away.

He straightened and rubbed his stomach again.

The phone rang. He glanced at the ID.

His hand clenched.

The goddamned police. Again.

CHAPTER 38

CHAIN OF ROCKS

"I still don't think we had to leave this early," said Tish. "It's a bridge. It's not like it's going anywhere."

Kat would have rolled her eyes if she hadn't been driving. Tish had been complaining since last night.

"Do you really want me to explain this again?"

"The sun is hardly up!"

"We went to the Rabbit Ranch for you," said Kat.

The previous day, on their way Edwardsville, Tish had suddenly pointed out the window.

"Kat, look! The Rabbit Ranch," she'd said, turning her head to read the small sign by the side of the road as they'd passed it.

"The what?" asked Kat.

"The Rabbit Ranch. We have to stop."

"You've lost me."

"The guy who runs it rescues rabbits. Luke's teacher talked about it, and he wanted to come. I pulled him out of school one day and brought him here. He loved it. I completely forgot about this. We have to stop."

"For rabbits?" Kat grinned.

"Look, you said this was a vacation, right?"

"I did."

"Well, I want to stop."

"Okay," Kat had said. "Rabbits it is. Point the way."

While Tish cuddled bunnies, Kat talked to the owner about his collection of VW Rabbits. She was particularly tickled by the half dozen of them buried nose down in the dirt in imitation of the Cadillac Ranch in Texas. Tish was more charmed by the headstone markers for the rabbits gone to bunny heaven where carrots were on the menu every day.

"Look. It's not going to take that long," said Kat now. "I just want to see it. My dad always talked about the crooked bridge. Then we'll go have breakfast in St. Louis."

"Fine," said Tish, crossing her arms and staring out the passenger window. "Whatever."

Kat frowned. "What's the matter with you? You've been twitchy all morning."

"There's nothing wrong with me. I'm fine."

"I don't think so. Something's bothering you." Kat waited for a few miles, but Tish didn't respond.

"We had a good day yesterday, don't you think?" Kat said finally, trying a different tack. "Our new story worked without a hitch. They didn't question our IDs. I think we deserve a small side trip."

"We're doing too much sightseeing," said Tish, fretfully. "We need to get on with this." She shivered as if she felt a chill.

"Tish... What is it?"

"I just want to get this done, okay?" snapped Tish. "I'm not comfortable with all the lying." She reached up and tugged at her hair. "I don't know why we had to wear the wigs. My head is sweating already."

Kat bit her tongue. Online, they'd found a couple pawn shops not far from the end of the McKinley Bridge, and Kat wanted to be ready to drive right to them after this detour. She'd already gone over this with Tish. There was no reason to do it again.

What she hadn't said was that if anyone saw them around the bridge, they'd remember a couple gray-haired women, not a redhead and a burgundy brunette.

Tish leaned forward to look sideways out the driver's side window, then sat back. "I don't like all these abandoned hotels and cafes, either."

"It's just a tired industrial area," said Kat, as they passed what was probably the last farm in the area, into an undeveloped area of woods. The road rose slowly to a bridge over flat plains on either side of a canal. On the other side was Chouteau Island.

The verge of the narrow, curbless road was neatly mowed, and backed by meadows and trees, some festooned with vines. Warm, damp air flowed into the open car windows, bringing the songs of cardinals to them. An occasional gravel road ran off at right angles, but the Buick was the only car on the road.

"I don't like this," said Tish. "It's kind of creepy."

"It's beautiful," said Kat, inhaling deeply. "It smells like summer."

"Smells like hay fever."

Kat looked at Tish surprised. "I didn't know you got hay fever."

"I don't. Luke does," said Tish. "This time of year is murder for him."

Kat was quiet for a while.

"You know," she finally said, "it's not that long a drive from southern California to Oregon. When we get to the end of the Route, I can drive you up there."

"I'm perfectly capable of driving myself," said Tish, peevishly. "But it won't be in this monster."

An offer to buy the Buick was on the tip of Kat's tongue when they pulled into the large circular parking lot at the foot of the Chain of Rocks Bridge. The wind whispered in the trees surrounding the lot. There were two cars parked on the asphalt.

"I don't like the look of this," said Tish, again, as Kat parked the convertible near the bridge's open gates.

"It's fine," said Kat with more confidence than she felt. She'd expected to see walkers or bikers. Not enough to be curious, but enough to give her a feeling of safety.

Regardless. She had to do this.

"We won't be here long," Kat added. She opened her door.

"Where are you going?" said Tish, grabbing at Kat's arm.

"I'm going to see the bridge, like I said."

"It's right there." Tish pointed across Kat out the driver's side window. "You've seen it."

Kat sighed. "I want to see the bend, Tish. It's the only bridge with a bend in the center of it. It's one chance in a lifetime. Besides. I've never seen the Mississippi."

"And I'm supposed to stay here alone?"

"You said you weren't interested in the bridge, and someone has to stay with the car, Tish. Remember what's in the trunk."

"There's no one else here. What if something happens?"

"You have your cell phone. And there are other people here. There are two cars sitting there." Which could have been there for months, Kat thought, but didn't say. Who knew how often police came through.

"I'm not comfortable with this."

"You'll be fine," said Kat. "Just stay in the car and keep the doors locked. Don't open up for anyone. I'll be back in about twenty minutes. I'll just toss my jacket in the trunk."

"Kat…"

"Lock the doors. I'll be back before you know it," Kat said and got out of the car.

"Fine," said Tish to the closing door. "Go get mugged." She went back to staring out the front window at the surrounding woods.

No sooner had Kat slammed the trunk lid than Tish began to worry. There were two other cars, sure. But who knew how long they'd been there? There were no buildings, no guard. There was nothing but trees, the bridge, and the wide, wide Mississippi.

A great place for a murder, thought Tish, then wished she hadn't.

Maybe it wasn't too late to catch up to Kat.

But that would mean leaving the car unwatched.

She glanced to her left, out the driver's side window, toward the bridge. Kat was just passing the big metal gates, folded back to allow access.

She was carrying the duffel bag on her shoulder.

"What the hell?" yelped Tish. "What's she doing with that?"

She wrenched the door handle, forgetting she'd locked

herself in. She twisted and popped the lock up, then shoved her way out.

Kat had disappeared onto the bridge.

"Kat!" she called. Her voice was swallowed by the trees.

"I'll kill her," said Tish. "Wanted to see the bridge, my eye. Kat!" she yelled again.

No answer.

She's going to meet someone on the Missouri side, thought Tish.

She ducked back into the car to get the keys. Kat wasn't going to leave her in this godforsaken spot with nothing.

The ignition switch was empty.

She stood up so fast she hit her head on the door frame.

"God damn you, Kat Merevec!" she said, not bothering to correct herself as she rubbed the back of her head.

She pushed the door lock down, slammed the car door, and immediately realized she'd locked herself out.

She had no choice now. She started across the parking lot after Kat.

KAT KNEW the Mississippi was about a mile wide under the bridge, so it shouldn't take more than ten minutes to reach the center of the bridge, walking at her regular brisk pace.

The first part of the bridge ran over the slough at the side of the river. Trees pressed up to the metal trussing on either side. The only sounds were her quick footsteps on the roadbed and the breeze rustling the leaves. An egret flapped slowly up from the muddy water in the slough, its white wings flashing in the morning light.

Tish's fears had eaten away at Kat's confidence, but the morning peace was beginning to restore her. It would have been more enjoyable if it weren't for her task.

Tish will kill me when she finds out, she thought. But there was nothing else to be done.

She shifted the bag on her shoulder.

As she climbed the hump of the bridge, she came out of the trees that lined the bank and over open water. The breeze picked up, making the damp air feel less humid. The sun glittered on the swiftly flowing Mississippi, and the smell of the river rose up to her. Kat's spirits lifted. She imagined what it would have been like to drive over this bridge on the old Route 66. She took a deep breath, filling her lungs with the smell of freedom.

Her pace quickened, and she smiled, anticipating the bend in the bridge over the center of the river. To be able to look upstream and down, right through the heart of the country.

She wished her dad was here.

Lost in her reverie, it took Kat a moment to recognize the thump of bass echoing down through the bridge deck and a moment longer to realize there was a matte black Chevy Suburban with smoked glass windows parked at the top of the bridge. The driver's door was hanging open.

She froze, her heart stuttering. They must have broken past the barrier on the Missouri side. There weren't supposed to be cars on the bridge. But that wasn't what sent her heart racketing out through her ribs. It was the five men around the car.

Even at this distance, she could tell they were not early morning nature lovers.

The two lounging against the side of the car were passing a bottle from hand to hand and laughing at the two hanging over the upriver railing either spitting or puking into the water below. The fifth, wearing tattered jeans and a black muscle shirt, was lying back across the hood of the car, leaning on an elbow, one boot dug into the dull black paint of the hood, his knee bent. He was sipping from a bottle of his own and watching the puking pair without a smile.

Kat could see the spiderweb tattoo on the side of his neck from where she stood. The shaved area over his ears and his arms were blue with ink as well.

Shit. They hadn't seen her, but they would the moment she moved.

No sooner had the thought slipped into her mind when the man lounging on the hood turned his head toward her. The sun reflected off his shades. Keeping his eyes on her, he sat up. He said something. The other two drinkers stopped laughing and looked her way. One of them said something. The other smiled.

Time to go, thought Kat.

She slid the duffel from her shoulder, grabbed the handle, swung it toward her left shoulder, then back to the right with as much force as she could muster, and let go. The duffel flew awkwardly toward the railing, clipped the metal, and went over the edge.

Kat had one last glimpse of the hood lounger, as he slid to the ground, before she spun around to run.

And crashed directly into Tish.

"What are you doing here?" yelped Kat.

"What are *you* doing?" said Tish. "You're throwing them the money!"

"I told you to stay in the car!" Kat yelled. She glanced back up the bridge. The hood lounger was starting their way.

"And let you..."

Kat seized Tish's arm. "Run!" she said, dragging Tish around.

"I'm not going anywhere…"

"Shut up, Tish! Shut up and run!"

Tish dug in her heels. Then some sixth sense of self-preservation woke, and she noticed the men on the bridge.

"Holymarymotherofgod," she gasped.

"Run!" said Kat again, her fingers digging into Tish's arm.

Tish's feet needed no more encouragement.

"Holymarymotherofgod. Holymarymotherofgod. Holymarymotherofgod…" Tish panted in time to their feet pounding down the bridge.

"Hey!" yelled a voice from behind them.

The two women suddenly found extra speed.

"Hey!" came the voice again.

"I'mgoingtodie. I'mgoingtodie. I'mgoingto…"

"Just run!"

Kat was an experienced jogger, but with the adrenaline pouring through her blood, and her heart flinging itself around in her chest, it was the longest half mile of her life. She prayed the whole time that Tish could keep up. And that neither of them had heart attacks.

They were both weaving and stumbling when they hit the parking lot. Kat had the keys in her hand before they reached the car. Shaking, she unlocked the driver's door and wrenched it open with one motion.

"Get in!" She shoved Tish in and pushed her out of the way as she crawled behind the wheel, jamming the keys into the ignition.

The Buick started like a dream. Kat hit the gas and pulled it around in a tight turn, rubber screaming and back end fishtailing, as she gunned it out of the parking lot.

Tish half lay against the passenger side door, wheezing.

"You threw... You threw... them..." Tish wheezed some more, "...threw them... the bag..."

In the rearview mirror, Kat saw the hood lounger stop, lean against one of the gates, then double over laughing.

CHAPTER 39

TISH LOSES IT

"He's laughing."

"What?" gasped Tish.

Kat looked into the rearview mirror once more, as she roared out of the Chain of Rocks Bridge parking lot. "The son-of-a-bitch is laughing!"

"What?"

"He thinks it's funny. Watching us run for our lives from the scary dude with the tattoos. That *shit!*"

The adrenaline rush washed down with a flush of anger was a brutal mix. Kat started to shake.

As soon as she could, she pulled over where a gravel road branched off the lonely two-lane bridge access road. The keys rattled in time with her heart, as she killed the engine.

"Don't stop! Why are you stopping?" asked Tish shrilly. "Keep going!"

"They're not chasing us," said Kat breathlessly.

"Of course, they are! They probably know we have more." She clapped a hand to her heart. "I can't breathe. I can't breathe."

Kat reached across and laid a hand on Tish's arm.

"It's okay. They're not chasing us, Tish." *The bastard's just having a good laugh*, thought Kat.

Tish didn't hear her. "Dear God. Dear God. If he'd caught us, they would have... would have..." Tish's eyes were wide with the terror she couldn't speak.

"He could have caught us on the bridge," Kat told her, her voice shaking with anger as her fear drained away. "He wasn't trying. He thought it was a joke, chasing two middle-aged women he could have run circles around. What a prick."

Tish stared at Kat.

"You know them."

"What?"

"You know who they are!" She jerked her arm away from Kat's hand.

"Know the... What are you talking about?"

"You know them!"

"Of course, I don't know them. How would I know..."

"You went there to meet them."

"What?"

Tish nodded, her face splotching with anger.

"You threw them the money. You planned to meet them and leave me in the parking lot with nothing. With nothing!"

Kat stared at Tish.

"That's what you were doing this morning. That's why you were outside when I came downstairs. You were putting all the money into the duffel bag."

"I was simply..."

"You planned this all along! Being nice to me. Getting me to sell my diamonds. Getting me to open that safe. Oh, yes. I see it all now."

"Tish, you are…"

"I should never have trusted you. Fitz is in this with you, isn't he? He isn't really marrying Hilary."

"Tish, calm down. You've had a bad…"

"How could he marry her? She's as stupid as they come. But he could plan this with you. Or maybe you're double crossing him, too. That's it! He didn't know you were going to steal it all from him, you and your ex-con pals back there. That's why you didn't want me to talk to him."

"Tish…"

"And now we're parked here. And they're coming, aren't they? Are they going to kill me? Otherwise, I could tell everything I know." Tish's voice had been rising steadily. "And you'll take the car and leave my body out here. Then you'll have everything!"

Kat opened the door and got out of the car.

"Where are you going? Where are you going!" screamed Tish.

Kat walked to the back of the car and keyed the trunk open. Leaned in.

Tish threw open her own door and stumbled back to the trunk, her legs wobbling under her.

"I won't let you get away with this. I'll go to the police. I'll run. I can run. I can…"

"Tish, look."

"I won't let you do this. I won't…"

Kat grabbed Tish's arm and jerked her around facing the trunk.

Tish shrieked. "No!"

Kat tightened her grip. "Look, damn it!" She pointed into the trunk.

"I won't get in there! I won't…"

"Tish," said Kat, raising her voice and shaking the other

woman's arm, "either you shut up and look in the trunk right now, or, so help me God, I'll slap you into the middle of next week."

In the sudden silence, the buzzing of the cicadas was shrill. Deep brown eyes, almost black with fear, stared into blue eyes on fire with fury.

Tish looked away. Into the trunk.

The carry-on bag lay open, all the money in place, the gemstone boxes open, the stone papers marching neatly in rows.

Tish stared.

Kat waited until her partner's breathing was mostly back to normal.

"It's all there, Tish," she said quietly. "I'm not double-crossing anyone. Not you. Certainly not Fitz."

"I don't understand," mumbled Tish. She put a hand out to steady herself on the fender. Kat loosened her grip but didn't let go.

"Why don't you sit down," said Kat gently. "I don't want you to pass out."

Tish nodded and let Kat help her around the side of the car and ease her into the passenger seat.

Kat went back around and got into the driver's side, slamming the trunk lid down on the way. Tish was slumped down, her head leaning back against the seat. Sweat ran in rivers down the sides of her face, and the front of her blouse was soaked with it.

"Do we have any water?" she asked weakly.

Kat got back out, pulled the seat forward, and got two bottles from the box in the back. She opened one and handed it to Tish. She wiped her forehead with the back of her wrist, then opened the other for herself.

Tish drank like she'd never had water before.

Kat put out a hand and touched her arm gently. "Not so fast. You don't want to get sick."

Tish nodded and slowed down.

They sat quietly for five minutes or more, the only sounds the cicadas and occasional bird calls. Not another car came down the road.

"I just made a complete fool of myself, didn't I?" said Tish.

"I think we were both just scared out of about ten years," Kat told her, pulling the front of her sweat-soaked tank top away from her chest. She blew a breath down between her breasts. "And we did a half mile in about two minutes flat. The Olympic committee should have been there."

Tish huffed in a faint imitation of a laugh. "No," she said. "I can't run. I think I levitated. That was nothing short of a miracle. I'm on the road to sainthood."

"I think you have to be dead for that."

"I'm not sure I'm not." Tish suddenly choked up. "Kat. I'm so sorry. I said such horrible things."

"Hey. Hey, don't," said Kat. She patted Tish's arm.

"I just... Yesterday when you were looking at the gold... Then today, I saw you take the duffel... And then when you threw it to those men..." Tish was trying not to sob.

"Tish. Tish," said Kat. "I didn't throw it to them. I threw it into the river."

Tish looked at her for the first time in ten minutes. "What?"

"It was the gold, Tish. I threw the gold in the river."

"The gold?"

Kat nodded.

"You threw forty thousand dollars' worth of gold into the Mississippi River?" Tish's eyes were as big as eggs.

"I threw away evidence that could have convicted us of a burglary," Kat corrected. "Granted, it was an expensive choice, but did we have any other?"

"It was gold, Kat!"

"It was a prison sentence," said Kat. "Or worse, a death sentence."

Tish stared at her for a heartbeat. Two. Then closed her eyes and nodded. Laid her head back against the seat again.

"You're right," she said. "Painful as it is, you're right." A moment more passed. "But you should have told me."

"If I'd known you were going to jump to such wild conclusions, I would have," said Kat. "But I knew you'd argue. That you'd want to hold on to it and think about it more. And we'd miss the best opportunity we had of getting rid of it: the Mississippi."

"The Pacific."

"Not without taking it out on a boat. And not without trying to get it all the way across the country."

"Are you always right?" asked Tish tiredly, not opening her eyes.

"No," said Kat. "I never know whether to turn right or left."

Slowly Tish smiled. "No. You never do, do you?" She turned and looked at Kat.

Kat took a deep breath.

"Tish, I know this has been hard for you. Leaving your home. Losing your husband. Taking this kind of risk. It's been easier for me. I've spent a lot of my life moving from place to place. I know you don't know me well. But if I were going to split and take the money, I would have done it when you went shopping the other day." She paused. "Just like you would have done it one of the mornings when I was out running."

Kat saw the look of guilt pass over Tish's face.

Tish smiled faintly.

"I guess the thought did cross my mind," she said.

"We're partners, Tish," Kat went on. "I think we both knew that in Fitz's office." She wiped her hand on her shorts, then put out toward Tish. "California or bust?" she said.

Tish took the offered hand. "California or bust."

CHAPTER 40

BACK AT THE BRIDGE

Ty was still laughing when the sound of bass throbbed behind him, and the Suburban rolled to a stop.

"Man, didn't you hear me yelling?" asked Card, sliding out from behind the wheel and walking up behind him. "What'd you run after them like that for? You could have run them over two, three times in the car."

"Oh, man," said Ty, trying to catch his breath. "D'you see those bitches run? Fuck, I thought they'd have a heart attack. Specially the fat one." He started laughing again.

"Yeah, well, you're really gonna laugh when you see what that old bitch tried to throw in the river."

"What do you mean, try? I saw it go over." Ty straightened up.

"It went over, yeah, but it didn't go down. Got hung up on that catwalk on the side. Spinner back there," he jerked his thumb to the back seat of the car, "climbed over and got it."

"You dumbass!" Ty hollered at his brother. "You're so

drunk, you fall in, you'd be halfway to New Orleans before you come up for air. Stupid shit."

"So," he said to Card. "What's that old bitch got that's worth so much Spin'd risk swimming to the Gulf?"

Card grinned. "Turns out, a lot. Hey, Spin," he shouted back toward the car. "Get out here. Show your bro what's in that bag."

Spinner crawled out of the center of the backseat accompanied by playful punches from the other two that would leave bruises. He staggered as his feet hit the pavement. He stood and swayed and grinned stupidly, holding out the bag.

"Well get over here, asshole. Don't just stand there grinning like you had brains."

Spinner staggered forward.

"Thought it would be good, Ty. And I got it." He held the bag out again. It sagged heavily at one end.

Ty grabbed it. "God*damn* fool," he muttered. He jerked the zipper down and pulled the bag open.

And stopped.

"Holy fuck," he said quietly.

Card punched him lightly in the arm.

"Gold, man. The bitch was throwing *gold* in the river."

Ty pulled out an ingot.

"Think it's real?" asked Spinner.

Ty felt the weight in his hand. "Oh, yeah. I think it's real."

"How much you think is in there?" asked Card.

Ty shrugged. "I don't know. Looks like maybe fifteen, twenty of these bricks? Stamp says it's an ounce. So maybe fifteen, twenty thousand bucks?"

"Shit man, we're rich!" said Spinner, still swaying.

Ty's arm shot out, clipping Spinner on the shoulder and knocking him to his ass.

"No, asshole. We're not rich. We gotta sell it first." He looked back at the ingot in his hand, shining in the morning sun.

"How we gonna do that?" asked Card. "S'got some jewelry store's name on it. S'got to be hot. We try to sell it, we go back inside. I don't know about you, but I'm not ready to go back there for a measly three grand each. I say throw it back in the river."

"No," said Ty, a smile spreading slowly over his face, as he rolled the ingot in his hand. "No, it's not going back in the river." He looked up at Card. "I know a fence can get rid of it."

WE'VE REACHED THE END OF ILLINOIS ROUTE 66, BUT IT'S JUST THE BEGINNING OF THE ADVENTURE!

JOIN KAT AND TISH AS THEY SEE WHAT LIES AHEAD IN MISSOURI!

Be notified when *The Missouri Run*, book two of The Route 66 Steal series, is released! Sign up here for Liz's newsletter, or at my website when you see the pop up!
To find my other books, visit my website, https://www.lizhartleyauthor.com/
And thank you for reading *The Illinois Caper*!

THANK YOU! AND A REQUEST...

Dear Reader,

Thank you for reading *The Illinois Caper*, first in The Route 66 Steal series. I hope you are enjoying Kat and Tish's adventure. Drop me a line at Liz@ LizHartleyAuthor.com and let me know what you think!

I'd like to ask a favor. Your honest review of *The Illinois Caper*—what you liked, what you didn't—can help other readers discover a new book or author. If you have the time, post your review to my author page at Amazon.

To help get you started, I've posted some guidelines on my website, whether you're reviewing my books or anyone else's. All authors will be grateful you took the time. I know I will be.

To see all my books, follow my blog, or subscribe to my quarterly newsletter at www.LizHartleyAuthor.com.

Again, thank you for reading *The Illinois Caper*. I hope to see you again on Route 66!

Gratefully,

Liz Hartley

ABOUT THE AUTHOR

Liz Hartley is the author of The Route 66 Steal series as well as two series set in the small town of Eden Beach, California: The Eden Beach Main Street Novels, and The Eden Beach Crime Novels.

Liz has worn jewelry and picked up rocks since she was old enough to stand, so she was probably fated to spend more than twenty-five years writing about jewelry and gemstones. She has both Graduate Gemologist (GG) and Fellow of the Gemmological Association of Great Britain (FGA) diplomas. It's no wonder that birthstones play a prominent role in her novels.

An enthusiastic traveler, Liz has lived and studied in Japan, traveled with gem and mineral enthusiasts to Brazil, journeyed to southern Africa with members of the Los Angeles Zoo (where she was a docent for five years), and made two "grand tours" in Europe. She has also driven Route 66 from downtown Chicago to the Santa Monica boardwalk.

She does not own a television but loves movies and will read just about anything that doesn't get out of her way.

Acknowledgments

Books are never a solo effort, and *The Illinois Caper,* the first book in *The Route 66 Steal* series, is no different. I am sincerely grateful to my beta readers, Maxine Cass and Lauri Martin, who read the first draft with care and enthusiasm. Their suggestions were invaluable.

As I have before and no doubt will again, I depended on Devon Monk, author of more than twenty urban fantasy novels, for her ability to see deep inside the structure of a story to what is missing. Her suggestions always improve the book. With gratitude, my dear friend.

The Route 66 Steal series would not have been possible if I had not actually made the drive. Anyone with the desire and the chance to drive the Route should do so. You'll never look at the US in the same way again. While there are many ways to drive Route 66, the turn-by-turn directions in Jerry McClanahan's irreplaceable *EZ66 Guide for Travelers* made it possible for us to enjoy the drive without the frustration of getting lost. I highly recommend it.

Thank you to Kim Killion at Killion Publishing for the delightful cover and for always getting it right.

Many gracious women of PEO greeted us, fed us, and made us feel welcome across the country: Carol in Spokane, WA (my first port of call on the way to Chicago); Sally and Nan in St. Louis, MO; Vicki, Carol, Sheryl, Sherry, Bobbie, and Susan in Claremore, OK; Sabrina, Deanah, Lauren, Sammie Jo, Sarah, Judy, Ann, and Karla in Amarillo, TX;

Mayor Ruth Ann in Tucumcari, NM; and Kathy, Ann, Margaret, Lynn, Laura, Bernadette and Lynda (with a number of spouses) in Santa Fe, NM. It was a pleasure.

Last, but not in any way least, the drive would not have been possible without my friend, intrepid traveler, and navigator extraordinaire, Gayna Morris, without whom I might still be circling St. Louis. Gayna deftly shifted between phone(s), iPad, itineraries, and our *EZ 66 Guide*. Without her, the drive would have been a heck of a lot less fun. Who else could I laugh with at the mere mention of the word "turtle"? Just remember, Gayna, what happened in Gallup, stays in Gallup.

Thank you all.

Liz

www.ingramcontent.com/pod-product-compliance
Lightning Source LLC
Chambersburg PA
CBHW070449200726

48293CB00007B/2144